THERE IS A TIDE...

Seventeen-year-old **Simar Malhotra** is a high-school student at Step by Step International School, Jaipur. Born and brought up in Delhi, she runs a NGO called Parvaah whose aim is to generate environmental and ecological consciousness. A course on Shakespeare and creative writing at Yale University in 2013 inspired *There Is a Tide...*

This summer she attended a course in International Relations and Social & Ethical Writing at Harvard University. She aims to work in the social sector in India, and pursue her passion for writing.

Visit the author at www.simarmalhotra.com and www. facebook.com/pages/There-Is-A-Tide/866447473384486. Follow her on twitter.com/simar121296 or write to her at author.simar@gmail.com.

'A brave debut novel, this is a young girl's coming of age narrative, woven into the life of everyday India.'

Gargi Rawat, news anchor, NDTV

'A deftly woven tale of family ties, ambitions and contemporary society, Simar's novel gives us a distinctive glimpse into the lives of today's youth.'

Sunjay Sudhir, Consul General of India in Australia

'Simar has penned a fast-paced, engaging, and spicy novel that stands out for its richness of description and imagination.'

Darpan Kalra, management consultant

'Her fictional realm is beyond her years and she's India's new hope in writing. A poignant social drama that is compelling, riveting and irresistible.'

Swati Agarwal, educational consultant

'A brilliant story…'

Dhiraj Srivastava, PS to Chairperson, Rajiv Gandhi Foundation

'Simar Malhotra tells her tale with great positivity and perspicacity. This story of a fight for justice told against the backdrop of a country seeking transformation is infused with a firm faith in values and a maturity that is refreshing in one so young.'

Sanghamitra Ghosh, Principal, Mothers International School

'A compelling read.'

Manish Agarwal, IFC World Bank Group

'Her prose is filled with wit, tongue-in-cheek humour and emotional power which makes it a sumptuous read. The strength lies in the sheer genuine thought and feelings.'

Varun Bahl, fashion designer

THERE IS
A TIDE...

Simar Malhotra

RUPA

Published by
Rupa Publications India Pvt. Ltd 2014
7/16, Ansari Road, Daryaganj
New Delhi 110002

Sales Centres:

Allahabad Bengaluru Chennai
Hyderabad Jaipur Kathmandu
Kolkata Mumbai

ISBN: 978-81-291-3547-6

First impression 2014

10 9 8 7 6 5 4 3 2 1

The moral right of the author has been asserted.

All the world's a stage,
And all the men and women merely players;
They have their exits and their entrances,
And one man in his time plays many parts…

CONTENTS

FOREWORD

Words fail to express the intensity of my pleasure in penning down this Foreword for someone very close to my heart. I had always known that Simar Malhotra had an intense creative talent, and one day, very casually, I suggested that she should put down her imaginative thoughts in the form of a novel. And to our pleasant surprise, within no time at all, she had created this wonderful literary piece with her untiring efforts and unflinching passion.

What do I say about a girl so young and yet so very talented? She's a bright star in the galaxy of our literati. She is profound and perceptive and has the ability to discern people and situations extraordinarily well. The steady, unfailing balance of reason and sentiment, the graceful, refined portrayal of characters without any artificiality and pedantic mythological references or metaphorical devices is what makes this book such an enjoyable read. It has all the elegance and style of an accomplished writer, with touches of irony and humour that are most exhilarating. It is no wonder that she received such a positive response from Rupa Publications for her very first novel.

Simar, at her age, is unparalleled for her skill in plot construction. She handles characters and events, dialogue and storyline with an exquisite and masterly touch, fusing all the elements of novel into one complete whole, interweaving them so finely that no strand can be separated. She is proficient in plumbing the psychological depths of her characters and in delineating the basic principles of human conduct. Her novel has been an effort to explore beauty and meaning in the confusion of living.

What makes this book so special is the sensitive way in which Simar has handled the entire story, reflecting the anguish of the parents and the family for a son wrongly incarcerated. She portrays the painful realities of life against which her characters violently struggle, testing their inner limits of endurance.

The inconsistencies and the follies of human behaviour, hypocrisy, pretentiousness, self-deception, and the red-tapism of the government officials have been depicted by Simar with perfect honesty and conviction. It is the disorder behind the apparent order that she tries to unravel.

The commonplace incidents and characters are so skillfully revealed that reading this novel is a delightful experience. What in other hands would be a flat, insipid, intolerable piece of utmost dullness becomes, in Simar's hands, a sprightly, versatile, gripping novel of enjoyable entertainment. There is a refreshing freshness in the style of her writing which is distinctly unique and enchantingly captivating.

Simar is just seventeen and it is unbelievable that craftsmanship of such a high order can be found in a girl of such a young age, and that too, in her very first novel. Simar's sparkling style, her lucid imagination and absolute freedom from pedantry and verbosity and lack of artifice are what will capture the readers' attention.

Vivacious, irrepressible and gifted with enormous creativity and imagination, I am sure that Simar will go places soon. No matter how exhausted and dispirited you are, read this novel, it will surely enchant and refresh...and motivate you to dream big like Simar did.

I am deeply honoured to invite you to make this book a part of your life. Believe me, you'll not be disappointed, I vouch for it.

August 2014   **Jayshree Periwal**,
                                        winner of Best Women Entrepreneurs
                                        Award 2011 by The Indus Entrepreneurs (TiE)

AS YOU LIKE IT

*I*ve always been my family's favourite. Perhaps because I'm the only daughter or unlike my brothers I'm not a prodigy. Unless it is the frailest child who is also the most loved. Arjun Bhaiya, the star-child of the house and five years older than me, is in his final year at St Stephen's College, Delhi University, studying Economics. We had always known he would make us proud one day. He embodies perfection and it is annoying how he gets everything right. With the correct proportions of sugar and salt, his lemonade has never tasted sour—Head Boy of school, captain of the college football team, heart-throb of all the girls of his batch. I'm certain that he'll become a politician someday. I see those radical streaks in him. He is already a committed member of the People's Party and St. Stephen's is anyway a politically active college. If you search its exhaustive list of alumni, you will find that almost half of them are engaged directly in politics if not in the bureaucracy. If the dharnas and campaigns that he organizes are of any relevance, Arjun Bhaiya should indubitably end up on the same list. He envisions a corruption-free India, an India where you don't have to hand out a five-hundred rupee note to the hospital in-charge to get yourself a bed during an emergency, or a few thousands to get a licence; where public privileges don't depend on your take-home salary; where the tax you pay for the repair of the road outside your house is actually used for that purpose; where the common man isn't just a pawn in the quest for power but has a meaningful voice.

I love Arjun Bhaiya more than anyone else in the world. He is my third parent, my best friend and the one person in the world who, I know, would not, under any circumstances, leave my side. He is like those typical Bollywood brothers who would surmount all mountains for their sister's sake. I wish that someday I could return all that he has done for me.

Talking about archetypal brothers, I have another, though not so perfect, brother. Daksh is in his first year at Hans Raj College. The only misfit (too caustic a word I know, but unfortunately apt) in our more or less perfect family puzzle would be Daksh. It's not like he's intellectually impaired—he is also a genius born out of my mother's womb, although this genius rarely showed on test papers; debates, MUNs and sports were more to his taste. Let's put it this way, compassion and affection are not qualities I would attribute to him. Even though he's my brother, he does not feature on my list of favourites. It's funny how two brothers could be so different. Daksh's only aim in life seems to be to surpass the achievements of Bhaiya. His intense competition with Bhaiya is evident for all to see. Competition isn't a vice. Healthy competition is an impetus that helps you move forward in life and achieve personal excellence. But the craving to outdo, not for self-gain, but just to be able to look down on the other, is troubling. Daksh can't stand anyone who is better than him. I don't understand; what is wrong with being number two? You don't always have to be on the top rung of the ladder. Even to an outsider, the wall of hatred that Daksh has built between Bhaiya and himself is palpable. Even though Bhaiya tries to to overcome the differences between them, Daksh simply rebuffs his efforts.

Then there's me, the little 'angel' of the house. I don't have much to brag about myself, being the usual girl-next-door. I'm not a genius like my brothers. Nor am I the school captain or the head girl. I'm well, just, me. I set small goals and please myself on achieving them.

Overall we are a close-knit, happy family, with only Daksh deviating towards planet 'Daksh Commands' now and again. Sundays were 'Dad's Kitchen Day' when only Papa could enter the kitchen to cook pancakes and *alloo paranthas* for breakfast and *rajma-chawal* for lunch. Every year during the winter vacations, we would drive to Corbett National Park in the hope of spotting a tiger, but sadly, in all these seventeen years we've only seen a pugmark! Papa does not have any siblings, just a large number of cousins, scattered across India, one of whom visits us every year. Mamma has two sisters, the elder one lives in Jaipur, while the younger sister is in the United States and both are the personification of affection!

Daksh and I had the usual mostly-fighting-sometimes-not-fighting relationship. But this was only at home. At school, it had always been weird. Daksh hung out with his 'cool gang', and it was sad how he never acknowledged me when he was in their company. I mean hello? I'm your sister; you share your freaking room with me! Now that he was in college, a new aura of arrogance had come over him. Always patient and tolerant, Mamma and Papa had never castigated or rebuked him for his bad behaviour. Although they never said it aloud, they were getting tired of dealing with him. It was obvious by their sighs when he didn't turn up at the dining table for dinner, or when he refused to turn down the deafening volume of the stereo screaming out Iron Maiden. At home, I was probably the only one he ever talked to; if at all you could call a 'hey' talking. But even this brief conversation ended when the talks about going to summer school began. Arjun Bhaiya had always regretted not going abroad for further studies. Very often we would discuss the prospects of Daksh and me doing college abroad. Bhaiya had friends who were studying in the US. Every time he met up with them during their visits to India, he just couldn't stop talking about the superiority of their education and how, just by being with them, he learnt so much. Arjun Bhaiya really wanted Daksh and me to get what he had missed out on. He wanted us to go for a summer programme to the US which would give us a peep into the educational system, culture and life in the western world.

'Rhea, Daksh, you guys are very lucky you have such an opportunity to expand your horizons. And Daksh, it's not late for you either. These summer programmes offer university-level courses and some of your peers will be college students. In my days, I was stupid. Even when I saw my friends filling out application forms and taking their SATs, it didn't dawn upon me that I had a chance to go. I was always so focused on my aim of getting into India's best, that I didn't even consider the world around me. Today, when I meet my friends, I see a spark in their eyes. A curiosity. I deeply regret not going overseas. Don't get me wrong, I'm not trying to demean the Indian education system. It's great too. But I know what I am and what I could have been. Here in St. Stephen's, supposedly the best college in the entire nation, I am nothing but a frog in a well. And it's not about what we're studying, but the society and the environment in which we are—they inhibit our growth. Take Mamma and Papa, for instance. They're very hesitant about this plan. Especially about you Rhea, because you are a girl. And if this is how our own family thinks, how are we going to revolutionize the world? People have to break free from such inhibitions—their irrationality and their orthodox outlook has to change. We are the youth and we have to take the lead.'

'Um, excuse me please, but weren't we talking about summer school? You and your 'change' campaign! It finds its way into everything, doesn't it?' I teased Bhaiya. He digressed so much from the topic that anyone who heard us would never, even in their wildest dreams, have imagined it to be a conversation on going to summer school!

'Oh! I'm sorry if I got off the track. The 'change' campaign that we're organizing in college is so much a part of me now that I think I'm getting obsessed! Anyway, what I'm trying to tell you here is that—'

'Yeah, we got it,' Daksh interjected. 'You want us to go for some worthless summer programme in the US. Well, I'm not going anywhere, so just stop the pushing. It's those kids who don't get into any college here in India who apply abroad. I'm well ahead of my league anyway. Moreover, we're talking about a summer session,' he continued, sneering at the word 'summer'. 'It's nothing more than a money-making racket. So now if you'll excuse me, I have some actual work to do.' And he marched off, triumphantly gloating over the fact that he'd just dissed Bhaiya, and made him the butt of his ridicule.

Arjun Bhaiya didn't react to Daksh or his comment. We had all become accustomed to his acidity. And it wasn't the fact he did not want to go. He did; he certainly did, probably even more than I. He was resisting simply because Arjun Bhaiya was keen that he should go. How could he possibly acquiesce to something Arjun had asked him to do? That was against the one and only principle of Daksh's life! To defy Bhaiya and to contradict everything he said! What drove this sibling jealousy to such a grave extent? There was a time when the three of us were inseparable; we were the three musketeers always troubling our cranky neighbours, the sole reason why Mamma had stopped buying feather pillows; we were quite a team then. And today, the way that thread's been broken, I doubt if it can be knotted back again. Agreed that when the hormones kick in, teenagers tend to become more agitated, their emotions exaggerated; this may have been the case with Daksh. But somehow I think Mamma and Papa also had a role to play in this. Arjun Bhaiya was always brilliant; and in the light of his brilliance, Daksh paled into insignificance. Daksh wasn't academically inclined. And in a typical Indian household, academic brilliance is the only deciding factor of a person's worth. His talents were hidden behind Arjun Bhaiya's impeccable report card. Our parents and relatives made Arjun Bhaiya look like paragon of virtue. For Daksh, it was always, 'Do as Arjun says' or 'Look at Arjun and emulate him.' I wasn't affected so much because I was a girl, I never compared myself to Bhaiya; besides I had other worries weighing upon my mind, the usual teenage blues. In his attempt to be noticed by Mamma and Papa, Daksh strived to be better than Bhaiya. That's when the intense competition and ego started kicking in. And I worry because ego and jealousy are the ammunition of the weak and insecure. They lead you only into a dismal, dingy ditch of darkness.

Daksh was so hardened by now that no amount of homilies or counselling had any effect. The façade of indifference that he had donned had become so much a part of his being that even if he felt the stirrings of some feelings within, he wouldn't admit it, neither to himself nor to anyone else. He had buried himself inside a cocoon of indifference and apathy.

Arjun Bhaiya came to me one evening while I was reading. 'Rhea,' he said, 'We didn't get to finish our conversation about summer school that day. Have you thought about it?' he asked expectantly.

'To be honest, Bhaiya, I haven't. I just don't know if it will be the thing for me. What if I'm unable to cope? They're college-level courses you said. Plus it is a hell of a lot of money!'

'Rhea, I know you can do it. You'll come back having learnt so much, just believe me! Who else are Mom and Dad earning for? And the reason I want you to go is because I want you to see the world for yourself. You've always been treasured and mollycoddled by Mom and Dad. You can't always be sheltered and protected. I think it's important for you to get out, be on your own for a while, just be a free bird. Let's just settle for a yes now.'

Bhaiya was right, I had been pampered all my life; a little more than most people probably. My whims and fancies had been catered to; someone was always there at my beck and call. Such indulgence had not spoilt me, but it had surely made me dependent. Now was the time to change that. I nodded and smiled even though my heart was thumping.

Convincing Mamma and Papa was a little more difficult because it was just me showing interest in the summer school. However, Arjun Bhaiya was persistent and eventually emerged victorious with the change campaign philosophy monopolizing every discussion. Mamma's elder sister, Jayshree Masi, was an educationist, and her expert views finally convinced my parents.

'Summer school is an experience which is meant for academically driven and gifted students. You share your classroom with university professors and students, which will probably be the best kind of exposure Rhea could ever get! So many of my students attend such programmes. It is a once in a lifetime experience!' Masi told Mamma. Then she said to Arjun, 'You must send her for a credit course, Arjun. Although it will be more daunting initially, by the end of summer, each second will become more and more enjoyable.'

Mamma accepted any advice from Masi without any questions. She knew how supportive and experienced Masi was. I was thrilled yet nervous.

The application process was quite a struggle. The thousand forms and formalities; the essays; the TOEFL; they all sucked the life out of me. But with Arjun Bhaiya's help and after long nights of sitting before the laptop screen, I finally clicked enter. Then all I had to do was wait for a response. I was overcome by a heady mix of emotions—nervousness and apprehension being the most dominant. Yet there was also a sense of eager anticipation. An excitement to experience another part of the world with people never encountered before. Despite the exhilaration, the probability of not getting through was a cause of great tension. One day while surfing the net, my Gmail blinked with an email from Yale.

Congratulations! We are pleased to inform you that you have been admitted to Yale Summer Session 2013.

I screamed at the top of my voice. Tears of happiness rolled down my cheeks. I was ecstatic! Hearing the noise, Mamma ran upstairs to see what had gone wrong. 'Mamma! I'm going to Yale in the summer!' I jived and twirled her around until her knees hurt. Daksh walked into the room. Taken aback by the singing and dancing, he asked crossly, 'What's going on? Why has everyone gone bonkers? Isn't this enough of a madhouse without needing to explicate the madness further by hopping about like animals?'

For a change, neither Mamma nor I took much notice of his vitriolic taunt. Instead I spun Mamma around with one hand and caught hold of Daksh with my other drawing him into our circle. He shifted his weight between his feet—that was the maximum degree of dancing that could be expected from him, outside his peer group, of course.

'I'm going to Yale! I'm going to Yale! I'm going to Yale!' The moment he heard the cause of the celebration, he stopped.

'Oh, so you got through Yale Summer Session, huh? Great, you get the fruit of Arjun's hard work; after all you didn't even do anything for the bloody application besides sitting and waiting. But whatever, good for you.' And with that caustic remark, he walked out of the room.

'Daksh, how can you talk like this?' Mamma shouted after him. But as always her words fell on deaf ears.

And the damage had been done! Just like that, so easily, he ruptured my bubble of happiness with his prickly words.

'Why does he do that always? Can't he ever be happy for someone else? First he has a problem with Arjun Bhaiya. Now it's me. What a killjoy he is! Freaking Malvolio!' I cried out.

'Rhea, you know how he is. Don't pay any heed to him.

We've tried very hard to make him see that this resentment will not lead him anywhere. All that counselling has had no effect on him; your shrieking and bawling won't either.'

'But he does it all the time! And I know why he's doing it. He never got a chance to go to summer school, that's why. And it wasn't anyone's fault but his own!'

'Why dwell on that now? Fancy! You're going to Yale, Rhea! To Yale!'

Papa was rapturous when he heard the news. He went on to announce this to all his employees and friends.

Many procedures had to be completed. An F1 student visa had to be obtained; health insurance had to be taken; a no-objection certificate from school had to be collected. There was so much to do in such little time.

Daksh, sadly, only proved to be an impediment. His taunts and belittling laughs did not help us in any way. A 'Don't tell me you can't go to school; you're going to Yale,' when I skipped school, or 'You can't even do that and you're going to Yale,' were some of the nasty remarks he came up with intermittently. But they didn't have much of an effect on me. So, it was a little unusual when his girlfriend, Aanya, who came home apparently to 'study', asked me how I felt about going away for so long. She told me how awe-struck she was when she heard that I was going to Yale. Her source of information was obviously none other than my beloved brother. But from the way she sounded, it felt that she had actually heard good things and not criticism from Daksh. Hard to fathom, certainly.

When it was time to book the tickets, Daksh backed out from going to the US. He didn't want to 'waste' his precious time gallivanting around the streets of a little village (referring to

New Haven where Yale is situated). No amount of convincing could change his mind. I was happy in a way. Staying away from him for a while would certainly do me no harm whatsoever. Sometimes I wish I felt differently towards him. After all, he was my brother and it was my duty to love him. But his actions only made him more detached from the rest of us and making an effort to open up to him was a pain.

Anyway, because of his obstinacy, one parent had to stay back too. Papa volunteered. Arjun Bhaiya obviously couldn't come because it was his final year in college.

As we moved into the month of June, it was time to start packing.

I crammed Delhi's entire stock of Forever 21 into one of my suitcases. On Papa's insistence I filled the other full-sized Samsonite suitcase with Haldiram's *Aloo Bhujia, Bhelpuri, Punjabi Lachcha* and *Nutcracker* along with more than twenty packets of Maggi. If all this junk wasn't enough, he added 'Ready-to-Cook' packets of *Daal Makhani, Paneer* and *Rajma*, my favourite Indian dishes. As if there was paucity of food in America! But according to him, *'ghar ka khana'* was something that I would definitely miss. Papa sometimes behaved in such an inexplicable manner! Anyway, the day came when we had to leave. With a heavy heart and moist eyes, I bid goodbye to Kashi Bhaiya, our cook, who had packed *paranthas* and *achaar* for us to eat at the airport (despite the embarrassment it caused, Mamma always carried food from the house when she travelled; she didn't believe in airline meals). Surprisingly, Daksh wished me luck, when I did not even expect him to say goodbye.

'Bye Rhea. You're going to Yale, not many people get that chance.'

'Bye Daksh. I know I'm pretty lucky I got through.'

'Yeah you are.' Then fidgeting as though he needed to go to the bathroom urgently, he said, 'I know I said Arjun did all the work, but you getting accepted is probably, well, justified. I mean...that... uh... well yeah I guess you kind of write okay-ishly.' He was so uncomfortable trying to pay me a compliment that I wondered how Aanya stuck with him. A slight smile creased my face. To end his torture, I added, 'Yeah I get it Daksh. Thank you, by the way.'

Well that was Daksh, he was rude, he was mean; yet eventually he would make up for it in his own way. Incidents like these showed that he still had some spark of emotion; it reassured me that the Daksh, who I used to ride piggyback on, could be rescued from his dungeon.

SUMMER'S TALE

*J*ayshree Masi and her husband, my Masa, were travelling to the United States with us. They had come to Delhi from Jaipur the previous night. Papa, Mamma and I picked them up from their hotel on our way to the airport, and the forty-five minute ride seemed to last only a few minutes that day. I was so lost in my thoughts that time just flew like a bird in flight.

As we reached the airport, a chill ran down my spine. Even though the Yale Summer Session started in two weeks' time, the feeling that it was actually happening was yet to sink in! Yale was a college I had only heard about through Blair's words in *Gossip Girl*. Never had I thought that I would be privileged enough to even visit it, forget about studying there. It felt so unreal! So wow!

I was going into the T-3 for the first time after it was built, and was very impressed by its structure and design. An airport was a window to a country; it was the first place a visitor set foot in. I was happy to see the progress India had made. Although it was slow, change was happening. We are always criticizing the government for its malpractices, corruption and general incompetence, but now it was time to give it some credit.

After completing all the procedures, we finally boarded the

airplane that would stopover at Amsterdam before taking us to the US. Sitting in the aisle seat, I lived in fear of having my head squashed under the weight of the overhead bin. I was certain that it would fall any moment because of the trembling weight of the bags stacked inside it. My backpack, having found no space above, was sitting at my feet. It was very noisy inside the plane, almost as if a thousand frogs had found their way inside. The children's constant crying and cribbing and their mothers' scolding and screaming made falling asleep a distant dream.

The moment the plane landed in Amsterdam, passengers started to get up despite the 'Seatbelt On' sign. This stampede in airplanes always annoys me. What was the need for this rush, I never could understand.

A rude shock awaited all of us at Amsterdam airport. A melodious British voice announced loudly and clearly:

'All the passengers travelling to New York on D877 are requested to please remain calm as the flight is slightly delayed due to unavoidable technical problems. Further announcements will be made to keep you informed about the situation.'

Further announcements informed us that the flight had been delayed by eighteen whole hours! So much for a 'slight delay'! Thankfully the airport officials arranged a night's stay at a neighbouring hotel. Because of the prolonged delay, we were asked to collect our luggage. Mamma and Masi went to the washroom while Rupendra Masa and I went to collect the bags. A large crowd had gathered around the conveyor belt, waiting for their baggage and from their irritated expressions it was evident that the poor airport staff was being cursed. Many of the passengers had been on the flight with us, though some were new faces. They were all flying to New York on D877. As

Masa went to get two trolleys, I stood by the belt cautiously waiting for the familiar bags to arrive. Still running on Indian time, I was jetlagged and sleepy when a black Samsonite bag with a neon orange ribbon was loaded on to the belt. I moved forward to pick it up, but soon realized that it was way too heavy for me to lift. A pair of hands suddenly appeared and easily lifted the bag to place it beside me. I turned around to see the owner of the hands. I saw two young boys, about my own age, standing behind me. They looked Indian; although I hadn't seen them at the Delhi airport or on the flight. They were both tall and strikingly goodlooking, a feast for the eyes. They had backpacks hung over their broad shoulders and a folder in their hands, probably carrying passports and other documents. The two didn't seem like brothers to me. One of them had a slight hunch, but his sharp features and smile that could melt glaciers more than made up for it. The other had hair falling all over his eyes, making him look like an Asian Justin Bieber. I smiled and said, 'Thank you so much. I wouldn't have been able to lift that one myself.'

'Yeah, we kind of realized that, looking at you struggle to move it,' Justin Bieber said with a warm smile.

'You are going to have to help me with the next few that come along as well.'

They laughed and nodded. They picked up my next two suitcases which followed almost immediately and four of their own. By the time Masa came in with the trolleys, we had collected all the nine bags. Masa also thanked the boys as they helped us pile the bags on to the trolleys. As we made our way through the swarming beehive, I asked them, 'So you're from Delhi too?'

They laughed, and shaking his head, Justin Bieber replied, 'No, no. We're from Islamabad, that's the capital of Pakistan, by the way.'

I was taken aback slightly, not because they were from Pakistan (or so I liked to believe at least), but because I had assumed them to be Indian. Their nationality excited me. I had never made friends with a Pakistani before; Indians and Pakistanis have never had the best relations anyway. Even Masa gave me a 'raised-eyebrow' look.

'I know what Islamabad is, silly,' I said, not letting my surprise shadow my expression or tone.

They chuckled in response. Right then, we heard the announcer's voice.

'All passengers who are travelling to New York on D877 are requested to assemble by gate number 14. They will be escorted to Hotel Best Western. The buses will start leaving in exactly fifteen minutes.'

'We're all headed the same way, I suppose?' the boy with the hunch said.

'Yeah, I suppose so.' I replied.

Mamma and Masi were waiting at the gate. A long queue was forming but to my great relief they were somewhere near the front. We quickly made our way towards them. I told my new friends to join us as well. Eyeing the two boys suspiciously, my mom asked me discreetly about them. Her delighted expression when I told her that they'd helped us with our luggage evaporated in seconds when I said that they were from Pakistan. 'Look at them, they didn't even come up and greet us. Talk about etiquette and courtesy! These Pakistanis!' I didn't want to have a fight with Mamma in public and especially not when I was leaving for Yale, but her comment really disgusted me. Just the mention of a nationality, a name, a community was enough to make her ignore the fact that they had helped us. Even though I was acutely aware of the prejudices that existed between both the nations, my mind, for a minute, couldn't fathom the reason why the Line of Control should extend beyond the borders.

The bus that took us to the hotel was packed with people. All through the drive, Mamma kept giving the poor boys dirty looks surreptitiously, but I was quite certain that she would have done so even if their heads weren't averted. I worried about how childish she was. India and Pakistan were cut from the same geographic and ethnic cloth. We shared the same history and culture, even the language and food was the same, at least for those of us who live in North India. So where lay the differences?

Another surprise awaited us when we reached the hotel. When we got off the bus, dragging bags that weighed more than our own body weight (well, at least my suitcase felt like that), we were told that there were no bellboys! We were so used to having domestic help back home that just the thought of lugging our bags up the steps made us feel tired. Just as Mamma began to pick up one of the bags, Justin Bieber came forward and said, 'Aunty, please don't worry, we'll carry them up for you.' He lifted the bag easily, ran up the steps and deposited it at the entrance. Rupendra Masa told him not to bother, and indicated that he could manage, but then the boy-with-a-hunch-but-charming-smile picked another, although with some effort, and told Masa, 'C'mon Uncle. We're like your sons, don't be so formal. If we all don't help one another, who will?' His words, though casual, hit me hard. Had he referred to Indians and Pakistanis as 'we all'? A sense of connectedness enveloped me.

After depositing all the bags at the entrance, the boy-with-a-hunch-but-charming-smile came to Mamma, Masi and Masa and said, 'We weren't formally introduced before, I'm Usama and that's Salar,' and they both bowed their heads in respect. 'It's nice meeting you.' Mamma and Masi said, charmed by their manners. Suddenly Mamma's inhibitions seemed to have drifted away. She would never admit it openly, but it was clear from her tone when she said that 'they were nice boys' that she regretted being judgmental. This is what we always do, judging people, harbouring preconceived notions about them without really knowing who they are. What right have we to do so if we don't know anything about them?

My supressed fear and anxiety returned that night, and I was tormented by my thoughts—what would happen if I couldn't adjust to life in Yale? What if I couldn't cope with the intensity of my class? What if people looked down on me because of my colour? My stomach gurgled for some weird reason and I felt like puking. Despite the air conditioning, beads of sweat rolled down my back. I was becoming claustrophobic, even though only Mamma was in the room. After tossing and turning for what seemed like hours in a bed that was probably softer than Mummy Bear's in Goldilocks, I made my way downstairs to the coffee shop in the hotel. I needed some fresh air.

When I entered the coffee shop, I spotted Usama and Salar sitting at one of the tables. They looked at me and waved. I pulled up a chair next to them and sat down.

'Not getting much sleep, huh?' Usama winked.

'You guys don't seem to be getting much of it either,' I retorted.

'We've ordered coffee, would you like a cup?' he asked.

'Smart people, drinking coffee when you can't sleep,' I joked. 'But I won't mind a cup.'

'Hey, we never got your name in the first place,' Salar exclaimed.

'I'm Rhea. You guys are Salar and Osama, right?' I said, trying to hide my snigger at the second name.

'Eh, it's Usama,' Usama said, putting special emphasis on the 'ooo' sound. 'With a 'U'. You people *woh* make me Osama Bin Laden!'

We all had a hearty laugh over 'Ooosama' and the similarity between the pronunciation of his name and the world's most notorious terrorist's name!

After several frivolous quips and jokes, we moved to the subject of our visit to the US. Both Salar and Usama were also going there for a summer programme, but instead of Yale, they were going to Harvard. What an interesting coincidence!

I returned to my room a few hours later and fell into a deep slumber, until the alarm jolted me awake. It was time to leave for the airport. Most of the passengers who were boarding the plane had travelled from New Delhi with us, but the queue was too long for me to catch a glimpse of Salar and Usama.

The journey was uneventful, in fact rather boring but unlike the flight from Delhi, there was a marked difference in how people behaved. An aunty in a red sari, who had earlier occupied even our overhead bin in order to accommodate her jars of pickles and sweetmeats, now quietly agreed when the flight attendant politely requested her to keep her hand-baggage under her seat and in her storage. The seatbelts remained fastened till the end. No one got up until the pilot announced that the plane had landed. Everything was civilized. Even I found myself, along with Mamma and Masi, behaving more courteously. It was astounding how our demeanour changed so suddenly. Is this because we were no longer on Indian soil and didn't want to embarrass ourselves in front of others? And so we implicitly follow all the norms of propriety and decorum and do what is right and expected?

❦

After a nine-hour flight, we landed in New York City. We bid goodbye to Salar and Usma at JFK and stepped out of the airport. The hour-long drive to our hotel was spellbinding. This was my first visit to New York and I couldn't take my eyes off the images that flashed by—the towering skyscrapers, the bustle, the sounds, the excitement. This was New York City. The city of dreams. We crossed New York University and I was immediately reminded about the purpose of my visit. Once again a chill ran down my spine, and the biting wind blowing in through the taxi's windows was not the only reason for my shivering.

When we reached the Sheraton Hotel, we found that our rooms were not yet ready. On Jayshree Masi's insistence, we took our bags from the taxi (there were bellboys here, thankfully), left them with the concierge to be taken to our rooms and set off to tour the city. 'Time is the most precious commodity and must not to be wasted,' is what Masi always says. Our hotel was right in the middle of Times Square. Seeing the Big Apple through Masi's eyes was exhilarating; it was like tasting an exotic fruit that only got jucier and more delicious with every bite. This was contrary to the law of diminishing returns which states that the first bite is the best and every subsequent one fails to meet the mark.

Masi ran five very successful schools. But the fact that she was an affluent entrepreneur was not why she commanded respect. It was simply her air; her state of being, that was inspiring. Masi says the reason the US was so successful had a lot to do with its governance and the people; unlike India, where the political environment was a major force that kept the country from progressing. The rampant corruption, the plight of the minorities are just some of the issues that need to be tackled. She believes that there is an urgent need for reform and change. But the corruption in the governance of the country is so deeply embedded that even trying to plough it out will leave behind thousands of seeds to be yielded. A way to check these seeds from perpetuating further must be devised. Of course, there are restraints like the People's Party, but to kill the pests one must ensure that the pesticides don't damage the soil. When I asked Masi about what the other checks could be, she mentioned the RTI—Right to Information—which was proposed by Aruna Roy who happened to be one of her very close friends. The RTI gave the common man an edge over the government and made it more accountable. As much of a check as this may be, corruption still seeps in.

As I strolled with her through the galleries of the MoMa, the first on our 'to-do' list, she opened my senses to what lay beyond the eye and scrape through the layers of paint in Dali's *Persistence of Memory*. I've never visited a museum and learnt so much about the history of art as I did in that afternoon. Despite her aura of dignity, Jayshree Masi had no inhibitions about devouring Ethiopian food at a street corner, or chatting with a Gujarati hawker about the life of an immigrant. Equally impressive was her uncanny ability to discuss the vintage of wines and their pairing with a sommelier at a fine dining restaurant. She knows how to walk with kings without losing the common touch. New York City and Masi are synonymous, both a perfect amalgamation of yesterday, today and tomorrow. The squares of New York all add up to give you the most enriching time of your life as you soar to the most dizzying heights that the empire of your mind can permit and beyond. The city is well organized with its streets and avenues numbered and placed at right angles, and Masi's mind cuts through the grid of New York City, like Broadway, and opens my mind to the various theatres of life. I'm so glad the apple was big.

YALE—MY HAMLET

The day arrived when I entered the portals of the Ivy League University that I'd only read about in Jeffrey Archer's books and heard about on American television shows. Mamma's younger sister had flown in from Pennsylvania with her husband and two kids just to drop me off. Ajay Masa had taken time off from work just for this trip. It wasn't that we needed them for anything, we didn't. Masi, Masa, Kanika and Abhishek—my cousins—could have easily stayed at home, but they made the special effort to travel all the way just for my sake. There was so much love between my mother and her sisters and I always wondered if even half of that could be transferred to the relationship between Daksh, Arjun Bhaiya and me. Mamma keeps telling me about the importance of family. How in rough times it is only your family and real friends who come to your side at once. That's why she keeps emphasizing, over and over again, on how we must cooperate with Daksh and that, with time, he too will change. We must learn what our priorities are. In our desire to move ahead in life, we mustn't neglect the most important people in our lives. They are our kin; we can't afford to lose them.

❧

I arrived with a baggage full of sky-high expectations and a desire to experience a whole new world. When I entered the gates of Yale University, it was as if I could physically feel a change in the atmosphere. The smell of the air was sweeter. The song of the birds seemed more melodious. The wind teased through my hair, and the leaves rustled under my feet as I walked into the campus. Remember the stereotypical hero in romantic Bollywood films, the grand entry he makes and how the camera focuses only on him, ignoring everyone and everything else? I felt just like that. Of course it was not so, but my anxiety over the past few days had led me to create this bubble around myself.

'High schooler?' A loud voice boomed in my ear, breaking my thoughts. We had reached the admissions office and a young college student wearing a Yale T-shirt stood at the entrance.

The young counsellor escorted us to the cabin designated for the admission of high school summer students. The official at the counter was a plump lady with red hair tied up in a high bun. She looked like one of those compassionate and caring nurses you saw in hospitals. She glanced at me and then at the number of people accompaning me. Looking bewildered, she asked, 'How many of you are attending the YSS?' The moment she said those words, I turned as red as a tomato. I had more than half-a-dozen people as company. 'Uh, just one, me,' I said, abashed. Gloria, that was the name on her badge, simply smiled and remarked, 'Then you have to be from India.' Despite my embarrassment, I laughed. 'I've been working for Yale for the past seven years and every Indian student I've received has always brought at least half of his extended family with him!'

'Our culture is such that we can't help but love our family

very much,' Masi interjected.

'How wonderful!. I haven't met my kid sister in what might be a decade now!' Gloria exclaimed.

And I live with my brother under the same roof, but don't 'meet' him much either, I thought to myself sadly.

After a hundred thousand official formalities were over, I received my Yale identification card and was issued a Yale net ID and password. Finally, I was given the keys to my dorm and the young counsellor Jesse, escorted us to my new domain, Calhoun College. As we walked through the campus, I was overwhelmed by the greatness of this institution. The Yale campus was completely different from New York with its incredible, dramatic skyscrapers. The ancient gothic structures completely blew my mind. Yale was a town of its own! Arjun Bhaiya was right when he said that Yale wasn't in New Haven, Yale was New Haven. Jesse introduced me to the buildings, the large patches of green and the streets we crossed. Calhoun College was at the intersection of Elm Street and College Street. The university had one of the largest academic libraries in the world and the second largest gymnasium. Arjun Bhaiya and Masi had already given me this information, but Jesse enlightened me further with the information that the Sterling Memorial Library was bang opposite Calhoun College and that the Payne Whitney Gymnasium was less than a five-minute walk from there. I promptly made a mental note that the library and the gym would be my most frequented places. Our final destination wasn't very far and it took us about twelve minutes to reach Calhoun.

Calhoun College had a pretty little courtyard, with lush green grass carpeting its grounds. Daisies, peeping through the emerald grass, smiled cheerfully in the mild glow of the sun.

As I looked up into the sky, the clouds seemed to form a weird curly bracket design. We approached Calhoun, and with each step I was developing cold feet. Yale was beautiful but there was nothing more that I wanted but to go back home and cuddle under my blanket. Nervousness and tension were making me giddy. But I couldn't say that aloud, not in front of my mother, or my Masis and Masas and especially not in front of my cousins for whom I had somehow become a role model. I was so nervous that desperation overwhelmed me. I needed something, anything, to tell me that this was the place I was supposed to be in; that I would be okay. The clouds did the job. The more I stared at the curly brackets, the more they seemed like an AUM to me. That was it. It was God's sign to tell me He was there; and that this was where I was supposed to be. This fake reassurance gave me the confidence to return to the world of the living.

I spoke to Arjun Bhaiya on reaching my college, and most of my fears evaporated after our chat. He was the best! 'I know what's going on in your mind,' he said. 'First thing, just remove all this anxiety from your mind completely. What are you scared of? Of not getting an A grade? It's okay, so don't get an A grade. Is anyone eating you up? No. You need to understand that failing to do something is okay. It's only when you know the sting of failure that you can you savour the sweetness of success. Right? Rhea, you just need to keep one thing in mind, never let this fear of failure stop you from doing anything. I keep calling you my doll, right? Well, be that inflatable doll, which despite being knocked down, always bounces back. You will bounce back too. However difficult, excruciating or intolerable things may be, don't ever give up. And now on a lighter but more important note, there is something that you have to do, and if you fail to do that particular thing then you'll have me to deal with. You have to, have to, have fun! You need to enjoy each and every second of your being there. Do you understand? It's okay if you don't submit an assignment, but you better attend that party over the weekend. Okay? That's all I want from you. You've gone there to learn and have fun, so come back having learnt and having had fun.'

I nodded and gave an almost inaudible 'yes' in between my tears. I was touched. These weren't tears of sadness or fear. Fear or distress didn't exist in my dictionary anymore. Arjun Bhaiya's words had made me more determined than ever; my family was not expecting anything from me, I had not been set any minimum standards; no criteria to be met, and that was exactly what motivated me to do something.

So here I was with my 24-inch Samsonite bag, carrying pants and shirts, shorts and skirts, some Indian goodies and a small iota of nervousness tinged with fear and excitement. But I had also come with a firm resolve to do something I had never done before, learn something new and go back empowered with that new knowledge. The 'what ifs' that had been hovering through my mind vanished and I felt more positive than before.

My big, fat family had drawn curious glances from people passing by. It was then that I realized that unlike most students of my age who had arrived by themselves, I had way too many people carrying my bags, trying to run errands for me and even helping me make friends. It was embarrassing. After a while, I wanted them to go, I wanted to do everything myself. That was the reason that I was in Yale after all; to do it my way. I politely but firmly tried to tell my mom that it was getting dark, that they could leave, but she was determined to feed me the *aaloo parathas* she had so painstakingly prepared. My cousins could not stop clicking pictures to send to the rest of my family back home. My fake plastic smile faltered and signs of frustration were evident. Just before everyone left, Mamma showered me once again with a gazillion instructions.

'Rhea baby, I know you're old enough now, but being the over paranoid mommy that I am, I just want to say what I've said many times before. Number one, don't walk alone at night, New Haven is a dangerous town with a high crime rate. Arjun's told you about the kidnappings and rape cases already. I don't want anything happening to my only darling daughter. Number two, but equally important is your health. You'll be here for over a month, you have to eat well, at least two glasses of milk and an egg every day. Only then will you be able to work efficiently. And if you go to a party, drink a can of Coke instead of what's being offered. You don't know people too well here and you never know what they might have added to the drink. Drugs, smoking, drinking, these are harmful practices. There will be times when you may want to indulge in these because of your friends or under peer pressure. But before anything, think for yourself. I have enough faith that you won't do anything wrong,' she said, turning away to wipe a tear. 'Last but not the least; you must respect your culture, your traditions and customs. You're here, so many miles away from home, to learn something new, something beneficial. Our society does not offer us too much freedom, but these restrictions are there for a reason and it is our duty to respect and abide by them. Don't get carried away by what others do. I know you're a good girl; it's your innocence that sets you apart from the others. Retain that innocence. Be rooted to your traditions and you'll be ready to face the world. I love you Beta.'

I didn't want to add to Mamma's anxiety and concern by looking sad or nervous in front of her. My unease would increase her apprehension and I didn't want that to happen. So with as much confidence as I could muster, I said, 'I'll be fine Mamma. You don't have to worry so much, I know my limits and I have enough discretion to know what is right and what is not, so just chill.'

Finally after a million hugs and more advice, I finally bid them adieu with tears in my eyes. I was excited yet nervous.

My dorm was in entryway C of the college. The three huge suitcases were sitting at my feet. Jesse, who had made himself scarce while the whole bye-I'll-miss-you session was taking place, emerged again. I couldn't thank him enough for helping me carry the monstrous bags to my room. I swiped my ID card against the detector, an act I found fascinating, and the doors to my-new-home-for-a-month opened. What I saw was not even remotely close to what I had fantasized about. My excitement fizzled away faster than a Diet Coke when poured into a glass. A very narrow and dark flight of stairs led me to the third floor where my dorm was situated. With only a single window on the way up and dim lighting, the staircase was dingy and depressing. A tangled mass of cobwebs covered the ceiling like the confusion in my mind. The eerie, gothic look of the campus had extended into the buildings too. If this was a shocker, the dorm's condition was capable of giving a heart-attack. My wing had only six rooms—mine was the last. The passage that led to my room was narrower than one in a two-tier Shatabdi and looked as if it was a storage room with tall lamps, broken chairs, wooden shelves and a sofa with loose springs. Jesse left me at the door to my room, wishing me luck for the summer ahead. Before I opened the door, I quickly recited a prayer, hoping that I wouldn't receive another shock.

It was a single room, spartan, without even a fan. It seemed to be just a little bigger than the double bed in Mamma and Papa's room. A chair was randomly placed in the middle of the room, lit up by a small bulb with a disgusting yellow light. The unlit fireplace added to the depressing atmosphere. And here I was expecting an inviting, brightly coloured room with sleek interiors. Considering all the classrooms and dining halls in the college had air conditioning, one would have expected the dorms to have fans at least, but this was not the case. How I missed Papa at this moment! My energy suddenly evaporated. Looking at the ceiling with a million thoughts racing through my head I decided to organize myself, putting my laptop on the desk, hanging clothes in the cupboard, placing a picture of my family taken on a trip to Istanbul, trying to make it look as much of a home as I could. Despite the disappointment, I kept my spirits high, making myself believe that it's not cement and mortar which counts but the real substance.

While I was in the process of unpacking, I met Krystal, the girl occupying the room next to me. She was the first friend I made.

After calling Papa for the eighth time and reassuring him that I was perfectly fine and that there was no need for him to talk to the authorities to allot me a bigger room, I finally got out of my little cocoon to explore my new world.

Although I had told Papa that I was well and had no problems or inhibitions, this was far from the truth. My heart was hammering and I was making a massive effort not to cry. Yale was a completely new place and I didn't know anyone at all. I was afraid. Afraid of not being able to make friends, afraid of not being able to cope with the curriculum. And most of all, afraid of letting my family down, especially Arjun Bhaiya.

Initially, I was hesitant to step out. I didn't want to look desperate or overeager by approaching people first. I didn't want anyone to think that I needed them in any way; even if I did. When I had aired these inhibitions to Jayshree Masi, she had simply laughed and said, 'If you need a friend, you will have to extend your hand first. Friendship is not like an a la carte menu for you to choose from, it is a buffet; no one will come to serve you. If the horse is hungry, he will have to go to the grass, the grass will never come to him.'

Thinking of myself as a horse, I galloped down the fatally narrow stairs from the third floor. I knew no one, apart from Krystal, and I wasn't very happy with that state. My premier mission was to throw myself out into the fray, to form a team of my own marines.

On the way, I met Amanda, a Chinese girl. She was headed to the bookstore to get a fan. A cute round face, small eyes and flawless skin, Amanda was very pretty. She was very outgoing, and after ten minutes of conversation, I knew her entire life story. Having nothing much to do and more than glad to have found another friend, I decided to accompany her to the bookstore and add the first sepoy to my army.

❦

Arjun Bhaiya had told me that most of the big universities had mobile applications that broadcasted daily news about the on-campus happenings, places to visit and a map to help one find one's way around. Because of its massive size, it was almost impossible to navigate the campus without a plan of the place. Bhaiya had advised me to ask around for a Yale application, if any, and download it. As we made our way across the Calhoun courtyard, I spotted two guys sprawled casually on the grass. They were in Yale T-shirts; definitely counsellors. As we got closer, and my myopic vision cleared, I noticed that one of them looked Indian. He was a handsome young man, with broad shoulders. His black hair fell haphazardly over his dark eyes and long lashes. His half-sleeved Yale shirt showed off his bulging biceps, not bulky yet enough to define their immense power.

Impulsively, I said, 'Um, hi.'

He looked up from the leaf he had been fiddling with and greeted me back jovially. He was cute, with small dark eyes. They were deep-set, kind of enigmatic, and when he smiled, the sides crinkled up.

'Is there any Yale mobile application that we can download to help us with the directions etc.?' I asked.

'Uh, mobile application? Do we have something like that Rick?' he questioned his friend sitting next to him on the grass. Legs outstretched unabashedly, his American friend said, 'None that I know of.'

'Yeah, I don't think there is any such mobile application,' the guy said, conveying his friend's message to me.

Definitely Indian, although his accent was completely American. Somehow I felt a little less paranoid about everything. It was funny how comforting it was to have someone from your own country around you. You don't know them, they don't know you, yet a sense of security, a reassurance that you're not alone prevails. Because somewhere at the back of your mind you know that there is someone like you, who's as far away from his culture, his traditions and his way of living. He's probably facing the same concerns and worries as you are.

Maybe it was because of this comfort zone that I found myself in or because he was simply easy to talk to, instead of simply accepting that an app didn't exist, I rattled on like a fool.

'Are you sure there isn't? Because someone told me that there was one. Yale's got a huge campus, how will we ever find our way around otherwise?'

'Well, for directions, you do have Google maps. And as far as mobile applications go I doubt there is one,' he said and laughed. It was a carefree laugh. And although he was laughing at me, he didn't seem to be mocking me. I felt foolish. Thankfully Amanda, who was giggling too, grabbed my hand, pulled me away towards the college gate and shouted a thank you to him. I don't know what was so funny about what I had said, but he continued laughing for several seconds.

Amanda and I opened Google maps on our phones and found our way to the Yale Bookstore. I wondered why Amanda had to go to a bookstore to buy a fan; I didn't say anything though, because I didn't want to sound sceptical. But when we got there, I realized why. The bookstore was not simply a 'book' store, it was a full-fledged super marche. From customized Yale apparel to books, from mirrors to toothbrush stands, everything was available. There was even a café. The bookstore was swarming with people. They seemed as new to the place as I was.

By the time we reached Calhoun, the Indian guy had left. It was around six o'clock. Amanda went up to her room to deposit her fan and requested me to wait for her downstairs so that we could go for dinner. I thought I had misheard her. Did she really say 'dinner' and that too at six o'clock in the evening?

As I was waiting for her, I saw a few other kids walk in with suitcases and bags. Only one of them, a Chinese boy, had his parents drop him at the gate of his dorm building. Everyone was so independent, so self-reliant; it was as if they didn't require anyone in their lives. I don't know if that was a good thing or not. Obviously independence is a desirable trait, but this display of not needing anyone can be a sign of disinterest, which is probably not so desirable.

Amanda and I walked to the Calhoun dining hall but found it closed. A counsellor, who was standing by the gate, informed us that Sunday dinners would be at Morse College. Now we had the task of locating Morse College. Just as we set off, another girl walked up to the dining hall gate. She was Chinese too. With glossy hair and glowing skin, she was wearing a short dress. She looked expectantly at the gate, before it was replaced with a confused expression.

'Yeah, we need to go to Morse,' I said putting an end to her confusion.

'Oh. Uh do you guys know where that would be? I've already gotten lost once, can't afford to get lost again,' she laughed.

Amanda and I asked her to join us. I felt a tingle of victory— this was another person I knew now. This may sound weird and immature, but believe me, being alone is the worst feeling ever. The girl's name was Moon and she was older than the two of us. Moon had already finished high school and attended a year's college in China, but as she was extremely keen to go to a university in the US, she dropped out of college. She was in Calhoun to take a summer course as a high school pass out.

It was a slice of good luck that, Moon happened to be residing in the room across mine. We hit it off right from the beginning. There was no initial awkwardness with her. She wasn't overly talkative like Amanda but neither was she too quiet. She was like me—sweet and nice (so much for modesty). Google maps safely directed us to Morse College. We were asked to swipe our ID cards when we entered in order to keep a track of the number of meals we had (we were allowed twenty-one per week). The buffet was huge. Lettuce and cabbage, tomatoes and cherry tomatoes, green olives and purple olives, cucumbers and carrots for salads along with ranch, blue cheese, vinaigrette, caesar, tomato sauce, barebecue sauce, cocktail sauce, mint sauce and steak sauce. A wide array of dishes, were available from Italian pizza and French fries to grilled chicken wings and salmon. And if this wasn't enough, we had six flavours of ice cream to choose from as well as brownies and cookies! It was an effort trying to choose what to eat. Even a moderate eater like me was tempted to savour all that was on offer. Moon, Amanda and I ate together, smiling and observing the bustle of the dining hall.

All the summer school students were asked to stay back in the dining hall for an orientation class. Effortlessly, the counsellors transformed the noisy dining hall into a formal conference room by rearranging the tables and chairs. As I ran my eyes over the many blue Yale T-shirts, I spotted the Indian guy whom I had met earlier in the day. I felt the same sense of relief and ease. Being out of your country for the first time on your own can be both exciting and scary and it's always reassuring to see someone from your own land. I had no idea who he was, but I found his casual demeanour and unrestrained laugh very attractive. Suddenly he caught my eye and waved. Mortified, I quickly looked away. He would think I was stalking him!

The Dean's speech thankfully interrupted the distressing flow of my thoughts.

'Good evening all you young, beautiful people! Some of you are here from nearby places and many from not-so-near places; I welcome all of you to the Yale Summer Session! I'm Dean Richard Stanley and I wish to make this summer as intellectually and culturally enriching as possible.' In his long speech addressing all of us aspiring Yalies, he introduced us to the police officials who would be on duty 24/7 to ensure our safety and security, the weekend in-charges who were responsible for planning activities and helping us unwind from stress and pressure. He went on to say that Yale University was different from other universities for it did not believe in producing just 'geeks' or 'nerds', but well-adjusted human beings who could meet the challenging demands of life. Well, hopefully, I would manage to become a well-adjusted human being too.

The World is my Stage

My Shakespeare class was scheduled for 9 am. I organized my bag for the next day before going to bed. A brand new notebook, three sharpened pencils and an eraser found their place in my Steve Madden bag. I laid out the shirt I would wear, matching it with a pair of shorts and sandals. I kept my undergarments, towel and toiletries ready, so as to not waste any time the following morning. I even kept a tablet of Ondem to prevent puking, and a bottle of water. Puking in the morning was a symptom, or rather an indicator, of my nervousness, a regular ailment I suffered from before weekly tests in school, a theatre performance, a party of the 'it' group. And since this was my first day without Mamma in a foreign land, an unfamiliar environment filled with unknown people, puking was a guarantee. The only fallout was the disgusting stink of the vomit. And to tackle that, I placed my deodorant and mouthwash along with the rest of the attire.

My alarm rang at 7 am, exactly two hours before class. I brushed my teeth in the bathroom that the six of us in my block shared. Thankfully, I was the only one there. As anticipated, the moment I finished brushing my teeth I threw up the previous night's intake. I brushed again, showered and got dressed for breakfast. On my way to the dining hall I met Amanda rushing down the stairs. The Calhoun dining hall gates were open and welcoming this time. All tables were occupied and the large crowd was making the hall stuffy. Amanda and I quickly grabbed a sandwich and some fruit from the elaborate spread and found a seat next to Krystal and Alan, Amanda's other acquaintance. I felt happy that I was getting to know a few more people.

The map that we were given to find our way around wasn't very helpful. I had received an email from my professor with instructions on how to reach Harkness Hall, but where on earth that was only God and Professor Leslie Brisman knew, I suppose.

With some help from the people on the street and Google maps (a certain someone had mentioned this to me!), I finally reached Harkness Hall. As I climbed the stairs to the second floor, butterflies began to flutter in my tummy. I felt like throwing up all over again. '*You'll be fine, just chill,*' I kept trying to reassure myself. I entered room number 215 and found about ten students sitting there, happily chatting with one another. I was late. Not for the class, but for the let's-get-to-know-one-another time. I was intimidated by the fact that I was the only friendless girl. I found my roll number, it was thirteen! My heart plummeted. Thirteen couldn't have been an unluckier number for me! Why couldn't my name have been Babita or Anita or any other name for that matter? I did not want to be roll number thirteen. If my earlier nervousness wasn't enough, my triskaidekaphobia (not really!) literally crippled me with anxiety. I hesitantly found a seat and placed my bag right in front of me on the table. I was the only Indian in the room, making me feel a bit of an outsider. I kept myself hidden behind my bag till Professor Leslie walked in and took his place at the head of the long mahogany table around which we had placed our chairs. He was very different from what I'd imagined. For starters I had thought Leslie would be a lady. I guess I'm not the best with names. Leslie Brisman had curly white locks and looked anywhere between seventy and eighty though his energy and passion was extraordinary. As he scanned the room, his eyes lit up with delight.

'Ah. It's such a pleasure to see so many young people interested in Shakespeare,' he said with a broad smile. It was his smile, or perhaps his congenial nature, but I suddenly felt more at ease.

'So, all of you are mostly high school seniors and college students I see.' I wasn't a senior, I was a junior in high school, but I kept silent.

'I heartily welcome you all to Shakespeare's Comedies and Romances. As the name suggests we'll be studying and analysing ten of Shakespeare's comedies and romances. But before we start, let's get to know each other. We'll follow the order of the roll numbers.' He sat back and looked expectantly at the class, the spark in his eyes even brighter.

A girl sitting near me spoke up. 'Roll Number One would be me. Hi everyone, I'm Alison. I'm a sophomore here at Yale University majoring in Economics. I've always loved Shakespeare, so I thought I'd study his works this summer.'

'Well, that's great to hear Alison, I hope you go back enriched and more in love with Shakespeare,' Professor Brisman smiled and signalled for the next speaker. All the others were either college students or high school seniors, and all were extremely smart. I was sharing a class with published writers, international-level footballers, musical geniuses and other supersmart Yalies.

I felt so small! I felt like a fool! My heart started pounding as Peter, Roll Number Eleven, started to introduce himself. I had nothing to say about myself. Why did I ever think that I could come to Yale and compete with such prodigies? It was a mistake, I now realized. Arjun Bhaiya was wrong, he didn't know anything; I simply could not match up to their level. Then it was my turn. I started sweating. My vision blurred, I needed water, anything. I couldn't say a word for the first few minutes till I heard Professor Brisman asking me to relax, calm down and a glass of cold water was placed in my hands. The coldness of its touch soothed me. My vision cleared. I saw Professor Leslie's reassuring face, his eyes warm with compassion.

'We have a little nervous someone here, don't we?' he chuckled sympathetically.

I went red as a tomato and apologized sheepishly, and then, as if propelled by some inner strength, I introduced myself.

'Hi everyone, I'm Rhea from New Delhi, India. I've just entered my junior year, so I guess I'm one of the younger ones here. I'm a little scared, a little intimidated. Unlike the rest of you, I'm not a genius, nor have I received any awards or medals of merit. I'm more like the regular everyday kid you'd meet on the street. I've never been so far away from home and that too for this length of time. But the fact is that I'm here and I'd like to imbibe and absorb all that I can from all you wonderful people. I chose to do this course because I'm in awe of Shakespeare! I am quite familiar with some of his plays, but I wanted to delve deeper into his life and work. So yeah, that's why I am here.' I had fixed my eyes on Professor Brisman the whole time. His eyes were warm and understanding. Suddenly I wasn't all that afraid any more.

The first class ended after the introductions and details about the seven-week schedule we would be following. We had already been given an assignment—an essay on *A Midsummer Night's Dream* for the next class. Arjun Bhaiya had told me that summer school would be hectic, but I never expected to be bombarded with work on the very first day of class!

Everyone back home was eagerly awaiting my call. During the course of the class I had received three WhatsApp messages from Papa. The moment I was free, I rang them up. Arjun Bhaiya picked up the phone, and then suddenly Papa's voice echoed in my ear. It seemed as though they were fighting for the phone. I felt good about that...desired and loved. Eventually they put the phone on speaker mode and I narrated all the events of the previous day and night and my class. The food, the size of my room, the hardness of the mattress on my bed, the kids living around me, the people I had met. Every single moment was explained in minute detail. I spoke at length about my classmates, their achievements and how small I felt before them, and about Professor Brisman, whose reassuring presence gave me the confidence to overcome my initial shyness. They told me about the happenings back home. Daksh was his usual stubborn self. Mamma was going to return soon. Arjun Bhaiya started off with his 'change' campaign and how tremendously well everything was going.

'Rhea, I can sense a change in the air. For once people are coming out of their plush drawing rooms, wanting to be a part of running the country. The response from the literate middle class is overwhelming. It's all so heartening! Once you're back, you have to play an active role too!'

Oh! I missed them all so much, it was crazy!

❧

We had so much homework that it was tough to find time to breathe! But I soon became accustomed to this hectic schedule. Sleeping for six hours was now a luxury that I rarely possessed. In those few days I read more than I had ever done before. I started spending a lot of my time in the Calhoun Library. Working in the dormitory was depressing and lonely. The next set of friends I made was in the library itself. Its prevailing silence and congenial ambience, friendly librarians and cooperative staff, and of course, the huge collection of books on fascinating subjects, written by eminent authors, held a million promises for us— students in search of knowledge.

ROMEO AND RHEA

𝒯he following weekend was the Yale Literary Social. All the summer students who were interested in literature, irrespective of whether they were in college or high school, were cordially invited to the event held at the Commons—a dining hall probably thirty times larger than Calhoun's. The YLS wasn't merely a literary gathering, it was more an occasion for like-minded people to meet and interact with one another. I was most excited. I put on my black Zara dress, one of my favourite outfits since it accentuated my curves perfectly. Its round neck gave me the opportunity to wear a tiny silver pendant that a friend had gifted me, and its low back exposed just the right amount of skin without looking too vulgar. I contrasted my dress with a pair of hot red pumps and outlined my eyes with kohl and glossed up my lips. I wasn't very keen on makeup to be honest, but I had this urge to dress up and look pretty that evening. Moon accompanied me to the social, though her purpose was definitely not interest in literature but the hunks she hoped to encounter there. Reaching the Commons exactly at 7 pm, we found two seats in the middle of a crowd of literary geniuses. An older but robust man addressed us in a sprightly manner.

'It's such a pleasure to have you all here! I'm Christopher

Blanker, Dean of Ezra Stiles College. Every semester Yale organizes a Literary Social to bring together literary prodigies to empower each other. I hope this evening will help you bond with people who have the same interests. You know what P.G. Wodehouse said, 'There is no surer foundation for a beautiful friendship than a mutual taste in literature.' This is what we desire as well. There's an open bar, sadly not serving what you'd like, but there's Pepsi and punch along with an elaborate spread of food. So enjoy yourselves to the fullest and make the most of tonight! But before I let you off to court your Romeos and Juliets, let's set the mood with some Shakespeare, shall we?'

Spontaneously, from somewhere in the crowd, a young man's voice rang out, 'Friends, Romans and Countrymen.'

Everyone looked in that direction.

'Lend me your ears.' Everybody, including Moon, turned to look at me. Without even realizing it, I had automatically uttered aloud the words playing in my head. Instinctively, I covered my mouth with my hand out of sheer embarrassment.

'I'll follow you and make a heaven out of hell,' the man's voice resounded in the hall. He paused. And as though there was some telepathic connection between the two of us, I spoke, slowly rising from my chair to locate the owner of the voice, 'And I'll die by your hand which I love so well.'

As I turned to find Helena's Demetrius, I saw the same Indian counsellor who I'd asked about the mobile application! He looked at me and grinned broadly. Those enigmatic eyes unnerved me and I felt the heat rising in my body.

'Such is my love, to thee I so belong, that for thy right myself will bear all wrong.' he said with a naughty smile.

'Sigh no more, ladies, sigh no more, Men were deceivers

ever, one foot in sea, and one on shore, to one thing constant never' I retorted back playfully. Everyone in the hall was gaping at us, thoroughly enjoying the show, as if it was a tennis match—looking at him first, then me, and then back again at him. The chemistry between us was obvious. But I was oblivious to what was happening around me, I was really enjoying this banter. No one I knew back home had shared my love for Shakespeare and literature. And here I found Mr. Hottie, who was also a Shakespeare aficionado.

Mr. Blanker, beaming with delight, exclaimed, 'The sight of lovers feedeth those in love,' throwing everyone into a laughing fit.

The Indian counsellor laughed too, shying away from the attention. He looked at me and nodded. To my surprise, a lot of people came up to praise me for my knowledge of Shakespeare. Many asked if he was my boyfriend. It was funny how they didn't buy the fact that I had no idea who he was. I really wanted to find my partner in crime, but he was nowhere to be seen till the end of the evening. As I was savouring the last traces of ice cream, a familiar voice called out, 'I do beseech you—chiefly that I may set it in my prayers—what is your name?'

I turned around to see the Indian counsellor dressed in a crisp white shirt and a black tie bowing down to me.

I cracked up at his gesture and said, 'Hi, people have been asking me where my Romeo is.'

'No! Don't tell me! And I am being asked to introduce them to my Juliet!'

We both laughed heartily at the stupidity of people. His eyes had great intensity and I found it difficult to break away from that compelling gaze. With great effort, I looked down at my red shoes. We stood there silently, and then he said with a hint of mockery, 'Those are... um.. nice shoes.'

I smiled involuntarily. Just as I was going to introduce myself to him, Moon pulled me violently to one side.

'What's wrong with you? What happened?' I asked, annoyed at being pulled away so abruptly.

'I'm sorry about that. But I think we'll have to leave immediately. I have a girl problem and I'm wearing a white dress,' she said in an agitated manner.

I didn't want to leave, but I was left with no choice. Moon had come with me for this event, the least I could do was help her out when she needed me. We turned towards the gate and started walking away when the Indian counsellor called, 'Hey! Red Shoes!'

I looked back and waved, indicating that I had to leave; we would meet another time.

❧

It was 2 am on Tuesday night and I was still in the library trying to complete my assignment for the next day. Fortunately, only the conclusion for the 2,000-word essay remained now. Having had dinner at 6.30 pm, the only thing that kept my stomach from growling like a dog's was the *alloo lachcha* that Papa had so thoughtfilly packed in my bags. At last I finished the tedious essay and was on the verge of leaving the library when a boy walked in. I was amazed to see someone enter the library so late at night. In an Abercrombie jacket and baggy shorts that fell down to his well-defined calves, he looked just a few years older than me. He looked familiar. As I turned around to check if I had left anything behind, I got a clear view of his face—it was the Indian counsellor I'd met on my very first day and then, a few days later, at the social.

'Hey! Mr. Shakespeare?' I queried.

'Red Shoes!' he exclaimed.

Mr. Shakespeare introduced himself as Abhimanyu.

'Where are you from in India?' I asked.

'Well, Varanasi. Dehradun, Varanasi,' he said bobbing his head first to the left and then to the right with indifference while mentioning the two places. A hint of frostiness edged his voice.

'So does that mean you were in The Doon School?'

He smiled warmly, his distance evaporating. 'Yeah, how did you guess? Do you know people who studied there?'

'No, it's just that you said Dehradun; it had to be Doon.'

He laughed in the same uninhibited way that he had when we first met. He asked me where I was from and what school I studied in. Then, quite surprisingly, he said, 'So you're here for the summer, huh? Aren't you glad to be away from that worthless land?' His earlier coldness returned, but this time there was a hint of something that I could only define as disgust. Worthless land? Why would anyone, and that too an Indian, call his country 'worthless'? India was not worthless.

'Worthless? Why do you call India worthless?' I asked.

'Well, what else should I call India? That's probably the subtlest word I have to describe the country.'

'Maybe you could do something about the worthlessness then? Make her a little less worthless?' I suggested.

'And become Father Teresa, right?' His 'I'm-too-cool-for-this-kind-of-shit' attitude was annoying. He seemed like one of those typical cynical, 'India-haters' who only knew how to criticize the country and ignore all her plus points. I decided not to pursue the subject. I was not keen on having a pointless argument at two in the morning, especially (not) with a person I had just met, so I simply faked a laugh.

'What are you doing here in Yale? I mean, you're obviously here for the summer too, but uh what work or study have you been, you know, engaging yourself in?' I asked, trying to structure my words coherently.

'Well, I'm a Yale student, and as for the summer, I'm taking classes for my much-needed credits,' he replied, sensing my self-consciousness and making a big effort not to laugh.

What followed was a very general conversation about who I was, where I was from and what course I was doing, until I yawned, signalling that it was time to go to bed. I said a bye to Amanda who wanted to stay on a bit longer. Just as I was making my way to the door, I offered him the *alloo lachcha* that I had been munching on. After an initial refusal, Abhimanyu took the packet when I told him that it would otherwise be going into the bin.

'Why would you carry food from India to the US? Don't you get enough here?' he joked. Once again, when he said 'India' the taunt in his voice was obvious. I wasn't a fan of people who hated my country which in this case, happened to be theirs as well. Anyway, I was happy that I had got to know a new person. Even though he was a little unusual in his dislike for India, he seemed like a good person at heart. Besides, we had Shakespeare in common which made up for everything else. It didn't take me long to fall into a deep slumber and I slept peacefully until my alarm woke me up for yet another day in the arms of Yale.

My perceptions of life, my priorities had changed since I

came to Yale. I could now fathom how different cultures and mind-sets could create essentially different people. Our habits and behaviour are so conditioned by what we've seen and experienced that it's important to travel to learn about alternate points of view and respect them. A place like Yale helps people from different places and cultures to find commonalities and is the perfect example of a shrinking global village. Moon, Emma, Franny, Nicole, the girls on my floor, are all from China. In the past few days we've got to know each other well, and have brought down the Great Wall in no time at all. I've discovered so much about them, their culture, their disciplined lifestyles, their strict parenting, so unlike my pampered upbringing. Honestly, no amount of reading could have given me such an insight into their world. The other day Nicole and I went to a Chinese restaurant and she taught me how to use chopsticks, a way of eating I was unfamiliar with. Back home in India we eat with our fingers to relish a meal, and no matter how unpleasant it may seem, we actually lick our fingers mopping up the last drop of curry. That meal provided me with much food for thought, far beyond the epicurean delights we had feasted on.

Although I'd been in Yale for only a few days, I could already sense the change in me. I had been told there would be work to do. A lot of work. And boy, were they right! From reading Shakespeare's plays to writing essays, everything was fairly new to me. But it was for these experiences that I had come to Yale. So after ranting, cribbing and crying for a day over the amount of work I had to do, I decided to go with the flow and do my level best. I wasn't here to compete with anyone but myself. I'm not a very ambitious kind of person; I tend to set myself small, reasonable targets and work towards accomplishing them.

So here too, I decided, I would do the same.

My family called me every night. After talking to my mother and brother, the phone was passed on to my father. Since he hadn't come to drop me off, he was more anxious than my mother about how I was coping. Initially I told him everything—what we had for breakfast, the temperature outside, what happened in class, my assignments and the friends I had made. But, as time went by, I didn't have time, immersed as I was by trying to keep pace with the supersonic course I was doing. Being an overprotective father, he's used to being in control and never misses an opportunity to check if I'm going out when it's dark, if there are any stray fellows who are bothering me, if I need more pocket money. I understood his concerns, that he was worrying about whether daddy's little girl was safe, sound and happy.

Sitting in the Bass Library, a three-minute walk from Calhoun, I had grown tired of reading Shakespeare's archaic 'thys' and 'thous'. *The Tempest* was developing a tempest in my own head. The peace and the calm of the library were lulling me to sleep, a comfort I could not afford because of my assignment. To rouse myself, I decided to take a stroll around the library. I nodded to Krystal who was printing out copies of her reading material. We made plans to go out for dinner at a nearby Chinese restaurant along with Moon, Amanda, Alan and Jacob, a high-schooler who was studying art. He was a funny kid. He had once told me how India and her poverty had intrigued him and how he longed to visit the country one day. I never realized that my country could be a tourist destination for such a reason.

I could see Range, another student in Calhoun, in one of

the individual study cabins, bent over his books. I felt like a nincompoop, roaming around the library while all the others were working diligently. As I was walking back to my place, resolving to get back to my books and not think about what I'd wear for dinner, I banged into the Indian counsellor. Libraries and Indian counsellors certainly had some connection.

'How fares my Kate?' he said.

'How dost thou, sweet lord, uhh, uhh. Ayushman?' I had forgotten his name! I knew it was a long one and began with A.

'Not Ayushman! That just sounds bad. Its Abhimanyu,' he corrected me with mock anger.

'Oops, I'm sorry. I'm not bad with names. Usually! I don't know how yours slipped from my mind.'

'That's not very nice to hear, I must say,' he said with a chuckle.

'I said sorry, didn't I? Anyway, how've you been?' I asked.

'I've been great, how about you? How's Yale treating you?'

'Yale's been an experience. Except for the workload we're being bombarded with, it's absolutely amazing!'

He laughed and said, 'I know that feeling. But you'll get used to it in a few more days, I guess.'

'Yeah. Hopefully I will.'

Then, suddenly, I remembered my plans for dinner and quickly considered inviting him as well. There was no reason why I could not do so, but I was afraid that he would think I was in love with him or something and was trying to chase him. No, but why would he think so. I was only inviting him to dinner, five other people would be there too, plus I hadn't given him any signs of being in love with him. I wasn't in love with him anyway. Definitely not at the very first sight! Why was I even thinking so much? Ugh!

'So all of us are going to dinner at this Chinese place tonight. Would you like to come along?' I finally asked.

'It's nice of you to invite me. But tonight may get just a little tight. There is a counsellors' meeting so it may not be possible.' Abhimanyu's excuse seemed genuine. 'But. But. But, how about tomorrow? Thou Lady, can I take you out?'

'Oh good lord, I'd be delighted,' I giggled.

'Great, give me your number and I'll text you.'

I gave him my number and the next moment I received a text saying 'Not Ayushman'. So Indian Counsellor had a sense of humour too. Not bad.

ROMEO AND RHEA II

*P*rofessor Leslie had checked all the assignments we had submitted the previous week. When I got back my paper, he had written almost an entire page of comments. While he appreciated my hard work and diligence, there were many aspects of the essay that needed to be looked into. After class, he had an individual session with me and explained what had gone wrong. Coming from a CBSE background, I was not accustomed to writing such long essays. Three hundred words were the maximum I had ever written. I explained this to Professor Leslie, not in an effort to gain points or make excuses, but to make him aware of the system back home. He was pretty shocked to hear of a system that didn't encourage writing. But he was very helpful, addressing each flaw and suggesting ways of overcoming them.

I waited eagerly for Abhimanyu's text the whole day, but that idiot never messaged me. It was upsetting. He had seemed so excited about the plan the day before and yet he stood me up. I hated people who didn't keep their promises. The rest of the day was uneventful. I had a long, relaxing swim and was more than ready for a delicious dinner of pepperoni pizza, lasagne and scrumptious chocolate-chip cookies. I was glad I had no other plans. But then why was I feeling so disappointed and dejected? I ignored these stirrings and put my mind to more constructive things.

Early next morning, right after my usual bread-and-butter breakfast, I went to the Calhoun Library to finish the reading I had planned for the previous night as well as what had been scheduled for the day. People weren't wrong when they said that Shakespeare was mad. His madness was driving me nuts. Just as the plot of *Much Ado About Nothing* reached its climax with Beatrice agreeing to marry Benedick, my phone beeped loudly. I could feel the reproachful stares of the other kids sitting in silence. The 'Turn off Your Phone' sign had clearly not meant much to me. I picked up 'Indians' from someone's audible whisper. With one beep of the phone I shamed my entire nation. Great! I checked my phone to see who had thought of me so early or late in the morning. It was a message from Abhimanyu.

    Hey! I'm sorry about yesterday. I got caught
    up in a lot of work and the plan totally
    slipped out of my mind. If you aren't too
    busy, how about tonight? I could show you
    around the campus if you'd like that, and we
    could grab some dinner on the way. How about
    I see you at 6.30?

Whatever little remnants of anger I was feeling toward him disappeared in a second. I replied immediately with a 'Sounds like a plan' and a simple smiley.

Professor Leslie's class was over by 6 pm. I rushed all the way to Calhoun as fast as I could. By now I was able to navigate comfortably between Calhoun and Harkness Hall and Google maps weren't needed any longer. A girl needed some time to get dressed and feel pretty. Not that I had to look pretty, Abhimanyu had made it very obvious that it wasn't a date. He had asked me to meet him at the Morse College courtyard, HIS college courtyard. Courtesy was clearly not a trait he possessed.

Deliberately taking my time, I reached Morse at 6.45 pm. Aanya, Daksh's girlfriend, always arrived a little later than the time she was expected. I think boys should realize that we girls have a lot on our plate and that they're not the end thing in life.

Abhimanyu was sitting on one of the deckchairs that lined the Morse courtyard. The moment he saw me, he got up and greeted me with a warm hug. We set off to explore Hillhouse Avenue. Abhimanyu told me that Charles Dickens, one of my favourite authors, considered it the most beautiful street in America. The green grass around the magnificent mansions resembled a plush carpet. There were birds chirping among the fig trees.

'This place reminds me of Kashmir. The fruits, the flowers, the abundant greenery…!' I remarked.

'Yes, though those flowers have wilted with the sound of bomb blasts and the stench of gunpowder, and the ripe peaches taste of communal discord.'

'But Kashmir is still beautiful,' I said in response to his sudden outburst.

'Of course it is beautiful,' he said sarcastically. 'Except that the polluted Dal Lake is no delight for honeymooners any longer. Every US citizen enjoys a sense of freedom, but Kashmiri civilians spend most of their lives under curfew. And what is your government doing about it?' Abhimanyu asked almost disdainfully.

'Many things have changed and are changing. Today, tourists roam freely in this paradise which lies in the Himalayas. The lake ecosystem is being restored. And as far as peace in the valley is concerned, it's all political. Abhimanyu, things are not what they seem at face value,' I said with an insight far beyond my years. Arjun Bhaiya and I used to have similar arguments. Abhimanyu was not entirely wrong; many people held such views, but they just had to be shown the other side of the coin.

'Mother India, *aapka Bharat mahan*!'

'Wow. You are harsh. Why do you hate India so much?' I asked. 'You've lived there all your life; and you've only been in the US for three years or so.'

'Why do I hate India? Hmm, let's see. The people are corrupt. The people are liars. They lie when they say they'll solve all your problems if you vote for them. They lie when you blame them for lying. They even freaking lie when they say they love sushi!' The veins on his temples were pulsating with anger.

I stifled a laugh on the sushi comment. It was so unexpected.

'Perhaps you should do something about the lying. Like teach them to be more honest?' I suggested. I found myself talking like Arjun Bhaiya.

'For that I will have to go back to *that* land. And that's really not on my wish list, you know. You can teach those who want to learn, not those who don't give a shit about anything.'

Abhimanyu and Arjun Bhaiya thought about the same things, but in radically different ways. Arjun Bhaiya believed in change, in the idea that people were essentially good and innocent; they just had to be made to see the wrongs they were committing and guilt would automatically guide them on to the correct path. Abhimanyu was less optimistic about the entire situation. This was basically the difference between a liberal and a realist.

'Someone is super cynical. No? How about we change the topic now?' I proposed.

Abhimanyu chortled, his eyes twinkling. 'I'm sorry if I freaked you out. I don't feel very strongly about many things, but when I do, I tend to get a bit over-emotional.'

He looked so cute when he laughed, I couldn't help smiling myself. 'I do want to know why you are so biased, *but*,' with special emphasis on the 'but', 'we'll save that for another day. Tell me about yourself. What year are you in?'

He chuckled again. 'You know you're unintentionally very funny.'

'Oh,' I said, a little taken aback. I didn't remember making any funny statement, even inadvertently. 'Why would you say that?'

'I don't know, there is something quite funny about the way you talk.'

Seeing my raised eyebrows and tight mouth, he quickly added, 'But funny in a good way. Anyway, to answer your question, I've just finished my final year, probably will find a job somewhere around.'

The question was more to give me an idea about how old he was than anything else. I quickly did the math. About twenty-two or twenty-three. Hmm...

We went to Shake-Shack for dinner after walking around the campus. Shake-Shack was the Yalies' favourite American joint after Louis' Lunch.

I loved Shake-Shack's motto: 'Friends who Shack together, stay together'. After reading that, I hoped Abhimanyu and I stayed like that too. Over the fries and burgers, the conversation turned towards our families. I told Abhimanyu all about my incredible brothers—both a little eccentric though for different reasons. I told him about Arjun Bhaiya and his passion for changing India, and once again we were back to the topic of India and why any attempt to reform the country would be futile and a wasted effort.

'Okay, so if you love your India so much, there must be a reason for it. Tell me what is it in that country that you love?' Abhimanyu's argumentative tone was a clear indicator that this would be a long debate.

'I love the fact that we have so many religions—'

'Which lead to communal riots,' he interjected.

'I love our rich history. I love our culture, its uniqueness and the diversity it brings with it,' I rattled on. 'I love the concept of family that we have and that you won't find here in the US. The support system it provides is incredible.'

'Not everyone finds support in their families. There are many times when family becomes a liability. It's the first brick that builds a wall, and if it breaks, the whole wall will fall.' For a brief moment, Abhimanyu's face exuded calm, but except that it seemed to emanate not out of peace but some inner disturbance. He stared at the ketchup on his plate briefly. Then in a jiffy, he shook himself out of his mood and his excitement returned.

'But anyway,' he added passionately, 'Point is, India is a crazy land! What is the literacy rate of India? Seventy-nine per cent. The budget allocates crores of rupees for education. Yet 304 million people are uneducated! Forget about education. Do you know that it is culturally accepted to defecate in the open? You talk about religion and unity, so why can't there be toilets before temples? Half of the 1.2 billion people in India don't have any proper facilities for sanitation. The annual tax returns of the government are over 93 billion! Not even half of this revenue goes into providing the people with basic necessities. Every third rapist runs free in a country where women are put on par with goddesses. This is the future of the country!' Abhimanyu had clearly done his homework, he wasn't, I decided, one of those 'I-hate-India-because-it's-so-dirty' kinds. As he paused to draw breath, I said, 'That's where you're wrong. This is not the future of the country. The future of the country is us, the youth, the *'yuva janta,'* as Arjun Bhaiya terms it. We have an edge over the rest—we are educated, the literate. We need to make that change come alive. Your criticism is of no use if you don't DO anything about the things you hate. I may sound rather clichéd but one must be the change they want to see,' I said with a meaningful look at Abhimanyu. Living with Arjun Bhaiya had made us patriots.

He picked up the menu that was lying on the table and hit his head with it in mock frustration.

Abhimanyu walked me all the way to Calhoun College. As I swiped my card to open the gate I said, 'I had a good time today. Thank you for the dinner.'

With great sincerity he replied, 'Frankly, even I had a good time today. I never thought I would, to be honest, because we are almost strangers and I don't find my name on the list of the super gregarious. But today was fun. We'll hang out again some time.'

'Yeah. We'll do that and you can rant about India and her pitfalls all you like,' I joked.

His eyes crinkled up and he bid me goodbye with a hug.

Just as he turned to leave he called, 'Hey, pop in a gummy bear before you go.'

'Random but appreciated,' I laughed extending my hand.

'I consider them lucky. These are special, you find them only at the Dollar Store,' he added with a wink.

'Yale graduate and lucky gummy bears, huh?' I mocked him tantalisingly as I made my way inside.

Saturdays and Sundays were always the best days. Not just because we didn't have classes but because Calhoun dining hall was shut and we went to have all our meals at Morse. The Morse dining hall was so much bigger than Calhoun's and the best part was that we could eat brick-oven baked pizza all through the day. From blondies and mini-donuts to New York cheesecake and peanut-butter cookies, we had a wide array of desserts to choose from. But the brownies and pizzas were not why I liked going to Morse. No matter how much I tried to deny the fact, the actual reason I liked Morse was because, after the library, this was the only other place I could meet Abhimanyu. There was something so magnetic about him!

Within two days we fixed up another meeting. I knew that Abhimanyu hated anything Indian, so I was pleasantly surprised when he took me to Thali—an Indian restaurant on campus. Just fancy! For my sake, knowing my craving for Indian spices and food and to make me feel special and feed my nostalgia! I was impressed by his sense of caring and understanding and my respect for him increased.

Only an hour had passed since the class began, two more remained. My stomach rumbled noisily. Thankfully it was a movie session and the volume of the video loud, otherwise I'd have been hugely embarrassed. How I cursed Amanda for my situation! It was only because of her silly date with James, the Italian photographer guy, that I had to starve like this! James was a summer session student doing a course in photography. I had gotten to know him after I modelled for one of his photographs. His topic had been culture. What could have been a better depiction of culture than a 'truly exotic Indian beauty'? I had carried a traditional outfit—salwaar-kameez—along with me, on Papa's insistence. It came in handy for James's photo shoot. Anyway, from that day onwards, Amanda had developed the hots for him. There was no doubt he was good-looking, his well-defined jawline giving competition to Tom Cruise, with perfect physique and rippling muscles. After hours of contemplation and discussion, she had finally gathered the guts to ask him out on a lunch date. But there was a condition. Funnily the condition applied to me, which in retrospect seemed so insanely idiotic, especially on my part, considering that I'd agreed to it. The condition was that I would accompany her to the designated venue and stay there (in hiding) during their date. As soon as I saw James and Amanda getting comfortable with one another over their pizza, I decided that this was the cue for me to leave. Sadly, it was time for my class and there was no way I could grab something to eat.

Because of the acute pangs of hunger, I could understand only a fourth of the film. *The Merchant of Venice* was one of my favourite plays, but even my interest in the tale could not make me concentrate. I signalled to Yvonne, one of my classmates who was sitting right across the table from me, air-rubbing my stomach and pulling my face into a sad smile. She laughed noiselessly. The next two hours were excruciatingly slow. Finally, the professor turned off the audio-visual and intoned, 'Okay class, it's been a great session today. I hope to see you all tomorrow, on time and maybe slightly more focused' he added, looking at me disapprovingly before he dismissed us. As if on cue my stomach gave a loud growl and everyone looked in my direction. My face turned crimson and everyone burst out laughing. Deeply embarrassed, I managed an awkward 'oops' and started giggling. Yvonne then said with a stifled laugh, 'I think someone needs to get some food in her.'

Just as I was leaving Harkness Hall, I realized that the three-hour session had made me miss dinner at Calhoun. Even though it was dark, and despite Arjun Bhaiya's warnings on New Haven's high crime rate and incidents of rape, I decided to find a place to eat on York Street. My sense of direction was still weak, so I switched on my iPhone and just as I opened Google maps, the screen went blank. I cursed Amanda for a second time that day. It was because of her incessant calls, that my battery was dead. Now my only source of navigation was gone. My stomach rumbled even more. I crossed the Payne Whitney Gymnasium and The Yale Bookstore swiftly, but as I went further, I realised that I was going the wrong way. I seemed to be making my way towards the Dollar Store instead of Yorkshire Pizza or the Fro-Yo shop. Yale's typical gothic structures had given way to buildings that looked like warehouses. There weren't many people around, and I suddenly came to the disconcerting conclusion that I was absolutely lost. A group of five men turned on to the road I was trudging along. They looked too unkempt and coarse to be Yale students or tourists. They were joking noisily amongst themselves, and something about their raucous laughter made me walk faster, to get away from them as soon as possible.

'Hey!' one of them shouted loudly. It was evidently directed towards me because there was no one else on the street. A cold shiver ran through me. I looked up. The voice belonged to a man in a sweatshirt with a hoody.

'He...hello,' I stuttered and scooted away even faster. The streetlight suddenly went off making me squeal loudly.

'Hey, wait up!' He screamed again. My phone was dead, I had no idea where I was heading—anywhere to get away from these louts. I could feel the fear building up in me. I continued to walk straight ahead, trying hard not to think about the kind of crimes Arjun Bhaiya had said were prevalent in New Haven. As I walked ahead briskly, the footsteps behind me also increased their pace. My eyes filled with tears. The distance between us kept reducing with each step. I tried to scream but my throat was dry.

'Now, now, now, is there any point in running away like this? We can be friends. Tell me your name,' said the man in the hoody in a raspy, gruff voice.

There was nowhere I could run to, no one I could call for help. I was only too aware that even if I tried to run, they would outdo me with ease.

'Please stay away from me,' I said, mustering up all my courage. I had been chanting the *Hanuman Chalisa* fervently in my head, hoping that some messiah, some saviour would come to rescue me.

'C'mon, don't behave like that sweets, come to daddy," one of them said, as they started laughing boisterously again. They moved closer and closer until one of them was near enough to touch me. He pulled the stole from around my neck. My heart started beating faster. I felt as though I was going to faint, not because of starvation but fear. The moment I thought I was going to collapse, I heard a familiar voice calling out my name. I looked up and saw the silhouette of a man walking toward us through the mist. My fear vanished the moment I saw him. I pushed the man away, leaving my stole dangling in his hand and ran towards the figure, clinging on to him tightly. A wave of security swept over me, though my heart was still beating wildly.

'Abhimanyu.' I wept quietly into his chest.

'Do we have a problem over here gentlemen?' His voice was courteous yet firm. I could feel the heat radiating from his body. His intense anger was very obvious, even though his words were mild.

Hoody-guy demanded, 'Who are you? This is our business; don't poke your freaking nose in what doesn't concern you.'

With one arm wrapped closely around me, Abhimanyu's tone was stern but composed, 'I don't suppose there will be any need to call the Rogers, will there?'

'Get out of the way, you scamp!' the man hollered and pulled out something that looked like a dagger. I let out a muffled scream when I saw it, but Abhimanyu instantly held me tighter and nudged me to keep quiet. But the man next to the hoody-guy immediately stopped him.

'Keep your mouth shut Randy, and put that away. Now!' he screamed at his comrade. To Abhimanyu he said as politely as he could manage, 'No, I suppose there won't be. We'll be making a move now. I'm sorry if we caused any problem here.'

And without another word, he and his mates turned around and walked away. I could hear the hoarse voice of the hoody-guy arguing with the sensible man. He turned his head around several times to give us dirty looks.

Abhimanyu didn't say a word but kept holding me till they were out of sight. Then he hugged me and kissed the top of my head before taking off his jacket and draping it over my shoulders. It would have been almost romantic had my heart not been thumping with fear. My tears subsided a little. As my vision cleared, I could make out the ripples of his abdominal muscles through the body-fitting T-shirt he was wearing. What was wrong with me? Why was I examining his stomach muscles at this time? He walked me to the nearest bench and sat me down next to him. None of us said a word. I leaned against his shoulder and burst into the tears I had been holding back. He put an arm around me and patted my head with the other,.

'Shhhh. Don't worry, nothing happened. You're all right, I'm here now. They're gone,' he pacified me. But strangely his comforting words made me cry even more.

'Hey, hey, hey. What's wrong now? I'm right here now; no one's doing anything to you. Give me one of those pearly-white smiles of yours now, c'mon?'

'What if he had attacked us with the knife? What would have happened if he had stabbed you? So much for the country you love. I could have paid the price of freedom today!' I sobbed. We had talked so much about India being unsafe; about the attitudes of the people who take advantage of a lone girl. But now I thought, what's so different about the US, a country we desperately try to ape? They say 'eve-teasing' is a word that exists only in the Indian sub-continent. I thought differently now. Abhimanyu lifted up my chin and tenderly wiped a tear rolling down my cheek and whispered, 'Did that happen? Why bother ourselves with thoughts about things that never happened?' And then he dug his hand into the pocket of his jacket that I had tossed aside and drew out a small packet of gummy bears. With a slight grin he said, 'It's these gummy bears that saved you tonight. Told you they're lucky. Open your mouth wide now.'

I couldn't help but smile at this and opened my mouth for him to pop in a gummy bear. That's when my stomach rumbled loudly demanding something to fill it up, and both of us started laughing as we made our way to the nearest restaurant.

'Hi Mamma! How've you been?' I yelled through the mic of my earphones. I hadn't Skyped with anyone from home for a long time. Usually we updated each other on day-to-day happenings on the family Whatsapp group, but audio-visual has its own charm. God, I missed them so much. Mamma was sitting in her favourite leopard print armchair in her room. Nothing much seemed to have changed in the décor, apart from a bouquet of flowers that added a touch of elegance to the room. I told her about my classes. I didn't mention the hoody-guy incident, knowing that she would have been flustered unnecessarily. Besides, I would have had to explain everything about Abhimanyu too. And that would have been plain and simple embarrassing.

'How's Daksh doing?' I asked her.

'Facebook and Twitter are working and his laptop's always plugged into the switches to charge so I'm sure he's alive.'

From Mamma I learnt that Daksh was his usual self. He had stopped coming down to dinner all together and was glued to the laptop. His girlfriend Aanya's visits had increased. But she was always welcome. Aanya came from a very good family, and every now and then she would bring along something small like doughnuts or cookies for everyone. She was our only source into Daksh and his affairs. She'd had more conversations with Mamma than Daksh had probably had in three years.

'How did Daksh manage to woo such a sweet girl?' Mamma asked, as both of us laughed heartily.

'Your other brother, I must say, has gone completely bonkers!' she said referring to Arjun Bhaiya. Apparently, he had been taking this People's Party business all too seriously. In the past three weeks, he attended college only once. Mr. Akul Nair, the founder of the party, had met him personally to congratulate him on his 'Change' campaign. This bolstered his confidence and passion no end, and organising signature campaigns, sitting on dharna and writing articles on youth participation had become a part of his everyday life now. Mamma and Papa were happy he was making such a difference in the world, but they were worried about him too. His dedication to political matters could someday lead him into grave trouble. 'Now he's involved in a very big protest that will be held at India Gate. I'm really scared, Rhea. He won't listen to us at all. Says it's what he was born for. When action heroes in movies make such grandiose statements they sound credible, but this is real life and he doesn't understand it at all. Perhaps if you talk to him, he'll slow down.' Mamma was getting worried as usual. She was one of those hyper kinds. So I said to her, 'Mamma, Bhaiya wants to be the architect of change. He has a vision to fulfil. Whatever he does, we'll be proud of him one day.'

Arjun Bhaiya had a dream to realise, that of a corruption free utopian society where the common man knows his rights and would not be afraid to fight for them.

THE TEMPEST

*I*t was a strange summer night—its sombre, solemn and spartan mood metamorphosing into a sudden severe storm. The atmosphere felt heavy and close, and the dark clouds had gathered. Unlike other nights when I would hit the bed and fall asleep instantly, I kept tossing and turning, feeling keyed up. The sound of thunder and flashes of lightning didn't help either. I hadn't called home for almost four days. I had been so engrossed with lectures, assignments and new friends that I had found it difficult to find the time to call my family. But I reassured myself with the fact that only a week remained before I flew back home. In my pitch-black room I saw a light blink on the phone. I thought it was Abhimanyu and grabbed the phone to find a message from Daksh. It simply said: Call back.

I called back immediately.

'Rhea?' he said. Something seemed wrong. There was a strange urgency in his tone.

'Daksh? Hi? How come you are calling me so late at night?' I asked.

I heard Mamma's voice in the background. She was screaming at someone to put the phone down. Was it Daksh she was screaming at? Why would she ask Daksh to put the phone down? It wasn't every day that we talked anyway.

'She needs to know.' Daksh said to Mamma, firmly but politely. Another shocker.

What did I need to know? What were they talking about?

'Daksh! What do I need to know? Daksh! Daksh? Hello? Talk to me, you idiot!'

I could hear Mamma's voice in the background telling Daksh that I didn't need to know. What were they talking about? My palms were sweating as though I was warming them in front of a furnace.

'Rhea, Arjun's in jail. And Papa's,' he paused, 'he's sick.'

My blood ran cold and my vision started to blur. I wasn't sure of what I'd heard. Did Daksh actually say that Arjun Bhaiya had been imprisoned? In JAIL?! No, I must have misunderstood what he said. My stomach gurgled. I felt a retching queasiness.

'Daksh? What are you saying?' I needed to be told that what I heard was incorrect. My heart was pounding frantically.

'Rhea, it's difficult I know.' His voice was controlled and steady. I could sense that he was making a massive effort to keep it that way.

'I'm asking something. What are you saying?' I said curtly. I didn't want to cry; I hid my anxiety behind a hard façade.

'You heard what I said goddamit!' He shouted into the phone. His anger shook me even through the phone. Tears came into my eyes. Like drops of rain on a windowpane, they pattered down my cheeks.

'Hey, I... I'm sorry. Okay?' Daksh said, regaining his composure. 'Arjun has been arrested. It's been three days now. And Papa collapsed because of the tension. But there's nothing to worry. The doctors say he'll be fine, just a little stress that caused it.'

I wasn't asthmatic but suddenly I couldn't breathe at all. The lampshade in my room started whirling, the dusty sofa was spiralling. Everything was spinning. I seemed to be stuck. Stuck by the horror of this moment.

'Arj... Arjun Bh... bhaiya is under an...arrest?' I stuttered. 'Why?'

Daksh sighed. He, who never hesitated before saying anything, who was so aloof, something must definitely be wrong to silence him.

'On charges of murder.'

I don't know what came over me but I started laughing. Guffawing rather. This was so outrageous. My own brother, a murderer? Nobody had cracked a worse PJ in a very long time.

'Rhea, I'm serious,' Daksh said. 'Let me call you tomorrow to explain what has happened.

'No Daksh. Tell me exactly what happened right now,' I said in a serious tone.

'A few days ago this major protest against corruption and in suppprt of the Lokpal Bill took place at India Gate. Akul Nair and other eminent personalities were present. Arjun was also there, protesting vociferously. But then, somehow, things got out of control. The police intervened and a riot ensued. Everything turned very ugly when they tried to suppress the uprising brutally. Some police constable,' he paused and gulped, 'Harilal Mathur, he collapsed and died in the melee.'

'Why was Arjun involved?' I asked coming to point. I didn't care about any Harilal Mathur or Thakur, dead or alive. My brother was all I was concerned about.

'He was one of the chief protesters there, the one who had brought in the most supporters.' Then Daksh added slowly, 'He was accused of murder.'

I was stunned. There didn't seem to be any rhyme or reason behind the police accusing Arjun Bhaiya. How could they even do that?

'What? They put him behind bars because they THOUGHT he was the murderer? What happened to evidence? What proof did they have?' Questions were racing through my mind. This was all absurd! How could someone, suddenly be thrown into prison?

'They've taken him into custody on suspicion. The bail plea has been rejected.'

I could hear my heart thumping.

'Now what are we to do?' I was so confused, so perplexed.

'You don't have to worry, just finish your course and come back. I'm handling it here.'

'What makes you think I'm staying here for seven whole days? I am returning now.' The composure I had tried to gather was lost. The saltiness of my tears burnt my skin.

'Shut up Rhea. Be practical. Don't even think about coming now. It's all under control here. I just thought you should know, that's all. Don't make me regret telling you this, okay?' It was hard to imagine Daksh taking charge. He was talking to me just like Arjun Bhaiya.

'And Rhea? Take care, okay? Don't worry. Do you hear me? Just... take care.' His voice was soft and steady; there was concern in it.

'Hmm. You take care too. And look after Mamma too.' I said and disconnected the phone.

The world around me had shattered. I got off my bed and crawled under it. With my chin resting on my folded knees, I wanted to hide myself. I had never been in such a quandary before.

Wrapped in my cocoon, away from all worldly misery, I fell off to sleep. I woke up to the sounds of rain falling on my windowsill and rolling thunder. It was eleven-thirty in the morning and I had overslept. There were three missed calls from Moon, probably asking me for breakfast, but I didn't bother to respond. I had more important things to worry about. Just then Abhimanyu called. When I saw his name flashing, I was reminded of Arjun Bhaiya. I needed someone to tell me that my world would right itself. I needed someone to turn to. There was no one except for Abhimanyu who I could talk to. I picked up the phone, but no words came out.

'Hey Rhea!' he said.

When I said nothing, he suspected something was wrong and asked, 'Rhea is everything okay?'

'Unhuh. Do you think you can come by Calhoun? Please?' That lump in my throat grew bigger. My voice cracked and my cheeks glistened with tears.

'Yeah, I'll be right there,' he said and hung up.

Abhimanyu arrived fifteen minutes later. It was still raining heavily, the sun obscured by oppressive clouds. My inner turmoil had become as disturbing as last night's torrential storm. I raced down to hug Abhimanyu; I was distraught but he was my anchor. My eye-liner was smudged all over my face, but I didn't care; nor did he.

'Ohkay,' he said, obviously taken aback by my emotional greeting.

'Before you say anything, let's get out of this place. I don't want to be surrounded by too many high-schoolers all at once,' he said, trying to humour me. No matter how much I tried to appreciate his attempt to make me feel lighter, I couldn't. We walked in silence to one of the benches under a tree outside the Bass Library, the only sounds being the falling rain. The rain fell like a million stars; destroying dreams and aspirations.

A tear began to form but I blinked it away.

'Tell me what's wrong,' Abhimanyu said. There was something in his voice, perhaps his reassuring tone that made me believe that everything would be better.

'Daksh, my brother! He called last night. He said... he said...' A flood of tears gathered in my eyes.

'What did he say Rhea?' Abhimanyu asked calmly.

I repeated what Daksh had told me. I was glad it was raining; at least Abhimanyu couldn't see my tears. I had never felt so weak and vulnerable before. Arjun Bhaiya and Papa were the two pillars of strength that our family was built upon. Today, both had been crushed.

'I don't know what to do Abhimanyu. I... I am lost.'

He gently put his hand on my back and for a moment everything seemed okay.

'I think you should go back home Rhea. To be with your family; give them the support they need. Summer courses will keep happening.'

I nodded my head in acquiescence. He was right; I should be home, by my family's side.

'Another thing, you can't keep crying like this. To be able to smile even in times of despair is the sign of strength. And you're strong aren't you?'

I nodded quietly.

'Don't worry. Everything will be fine. It has to right itself at the end of the day, and if it doesn't, well, then, its not the end so soon. Plus your eye-liner has smudged to such a degree that you look scary,' he said nudging me. 'So stop this *rona*, and pop in a gummy bear, here.' He pulled out a packet of gummy bears from his pocket and offered one. He took me in his arms and held me firmly, shielding me from the horrors of the day. I felt safe and warm, despite the cold rain. There was no need for any words. Perhaps everything would be okay soon. It wasn't the end yet.

Back in my dorm, I called Daksh on his mobile. I had to pack all my stuff too. Four rings, five rings... ten rings and he still didn't answer. I could hear my heart beating in my chest.

'Rhea! Hey,' he said in a flustered, hurried voice.

'Is everything okay? What happened?' I asked anxiously.

'Uh, yeah. All's okay. Papa was just a little uneasy, so we took him to the hospital. But nothing to worry about.' It seemed as though he was trying to convince himself while saying this to me. Strangely I didn't want to know more. I wanted to believe that there wasn't anything to worry about. I hated myself for wanting to shut out the pain.

'Daksh, I'm coming back home on the first flight.'

'I told you not to do so, right? Why are you being so adamant?'

'I want to come! I can't leave you and Mamma alone at a time like this.'

'Rhea, do you think that this is what Arjun would want

you to do? Would Arjun or Papa want you to leave your course incomplete? Especially when it's almost over?'

'I...' I didn't know what to say.

'They won't. Rather they'll blame themselves and bear that scar forever.'

'But Daksh, you can't possibly handle it all by yourself.'

'You have no idea about my potential Rhea,' he quipped. 'Just concentrate there and chill.'

'Okay,' I said reluctantly. It was Arjun Bhaiya's dream to send me here. He would never want me to return midway. And anyway, I told myself, it was only for a few more days. Then I'd be leaving anyway. All would be good; all would be fine.

'I want to talk to Mamma,' I said.

'Hold on, let me get her on the line,' he replied.

The situation was deplorable, but somewhere in the inner recesses of my mind, I smiled; smiled at Daksh's complete transformation from an uncaring brat to a responsible son, fulfilling his filial obligations. Maybe the effort to get Arjun Bhaiya out of jail would help Daksh escape from his self-imposed dungeon.

I could hear slight whispers in the background. It wasn't a quarrel, but I could hear Daksh and Mamma arguing. Then Mamma's frail voice came on line.

'How are you doing Rhea?' Her voice was devoid of any energy or emotion. That animated voice which used to be my alarm in the morning on school days sounded comatose and dead, aloof and distant. I clutched the phone closer to my ear in an attempt to get closer to home, to Mamma.

'I'm okay, Mamma. How are you doing? Are you... okay?' I was trying very hard to keep myself from sobbing. Before she could answer, Daksh took the phone from her. He told me she was a little unstable at the moment, but reassured me that there was nothing to be afraid about.

And then there was a tempest raging within me.

MUCH ADO ABOUT EVERYTHING

$\mathcal{T}$he week passed slowly. The thought of what was happening back home made each waking moment painful. Although Daksh kept reiterating that all was well, I knew it was only to reassure me. The day came when I packed my bags and set off for home. I bid a sad goodbye to Abhimanyu and promised to keep in touch with him.

I didn't get a wink of sleep during the entire journey from New York to Amsterdam and then from Amsterdam to New Delhi. I just wanted to get back home as soon as possible. Not that keeping awake would have got me back faster, but it just gave me a better estimate of the time remaining to get home. When I was home we would all figure out what to do. Even Papa would improve.

Daksh and the driver had come to the airport to pick me up. As I walked out of Gate Number 3, I saw Daksh at Costa Coffee, quietly sipping coffee. His eyes were staring into space, not wavering at all. When I called out to him, he turned, a little startled. 'Oh, Rhea. Hey,' he said and hugged me. It was an awkward hug—we hadn't hugged each other in ages. He took charge of the trolley with my two cumbersome suitcases and we moved towards the car. Then he gave me a detailed account about all that had taken place in the last two weeks.

D.P. Singh, who had been appointed the Commissioner of Police earlier in the year, also happened to be the son-in-law of Rajaji, a very powerful leader of the Hindustan Party. As the Minister of New and Renewable Energy, Rajaji had made hundreds of crores of rupees enough to keep his family comfortable for the next few decades. The People's Party had been fervently protesting against corruption and was on the verge of disclosing a list of all corrupt politicians and their scams. Rajaji topped that list, not only because of the money he had made but also for his abuse of human rights. We had heard several stories about him; one about a socially-conscious man, who under the RTI Act, asked for an account of how the money allotted for the electrification of his village had been spent. Two days later, the social activist was mowed down by a truck when he was returning home from work. The police, being hand-in-glove with the politicians, claimed it was an accident. But there was more than what met the eye.

As we were approaching home, Daksh said, 'Oh Rhea, I completely forgot about one thing. Just don't be too shocked when you reach home, okay?'

'Why??' I asked, wondering what was left to surprise me now.

'Bittu Chachi and Sonu Chacha are here,' he said grimly and got out of the car leaving me in utter distress over his last statement.

'What? Why? Couldn't you have told me before?' I screamed out after him.

Why was Bittu Chachi here? Why at this critical time of

our lives? Couldn't she have descended on us at a later time?

I entered the house with hesitation. I took off my shoes, tiptoeing silently through the house. It was eleven-thirty at night, they were probably sleeping, and I wanted to take all precautions not to wake them. Sonu Chacha was a turbaned Sikh and Papa's cousin. I know it sounds disrespectful, but no one could be a bigger pain than the two of them. They lived in Bhatinda and paid us an annual visit, just when the summer vacation was over and it was time to get down to some serious studying. They took the phrase, '*apna hi ghar samjho ji*', very literally and no amount of subtle hints could budge them. They were the true definition of crazy.

As I entered, Daksh motioned to me to keep quiet with a finger-on-the-lips gesture. Yes! That meant Chacha and Chachi were sleeping!

Kashi Bhaiya had prepared my favourite *rajma chawal* and Mamma had made visible efforts to make the house seem normal despite the havoc our wonderful guests must have caused. When Mamma saw me, she gave me the warmest of hugs and a big kiss on my cheek. Countless sleepless nights had obviously caught up with her and she looked extremely tired and frail. There were dark circles under her eyes, her spotless skin looked brittle and wrinkled, and her hair, which had always invited a million compliments, fell dull and lustreless down her back.

Daksh had already warned me not to talk about Bhaiya in front of Mamma.

'Where's Papa?' I asked, and Daksh immediately nudged me. I had assumed that Papa would be at home, lying in bed with high blood pressure or something. So, instinctively I said, 'What?'

Mamma looked up and said, 'He's in AIIMS hospital.' And with a forced smile she added, 'We'll go and see him tomorrow. First, let's all have some dinner. I'm sure not a single morsel of food has gone down there,' she said, pointing to my stomach.

We ate in silence. I developed a knot in my tummy and wanted to puke. Mamma ate a few spoonfuls of rice. The signs of depression were very evident. I looked at Daksh meaningfully, but he shook his head, implying that I just let it be.

'Mom? You must be tired; I think you should go to bed. I'll sit with Rhea, ask her about her time at Yale. Please go and sleep.' Daksh was composed. He talked very slowly, making each word clear and distinct.

Mamma was absorbed in her own world. She didn't hear a single word Daksh had said.

'Mom?' He repeated, a little louder.

Startled, she looked up in surprise. 'Yes?'

'I said, I think you should go to bed. Rhea is with me, don't worry. Besides Chacha and Chachi hardly leave you in peace during the day.'

I smiled happily at her, nodding my head in acquiescence.

She smiled and left the table. Without another word, without resisting even once, she just got up and left.

'Daksh, what has happened to Papa? You never told me,' I inquired.

'He's uh… he's in temporary coma, Rhea.'

My wide-eyed expression revealed my shock. 'But, it isn't very serious. The doctors say this is common among middle-aged men. He will be fine. Plus he is responding very well to the treatment. So, don't worry.'

Daksh had turned over a completely new leaf. His

mean, arrogant disposition had been transformed into one of compassion, sympathy and patience. I would never have imagined that Daksh of all people could behave in such a mature way about the whole matter. Even Arjun Bhaiya may not have been able to handle the situation as well as he did.

'What will we do Daksh?' My strong façade was crumbling.

'Rhea, whatever we do, crying won't help. So let's decide not to cry! Can we do that? Please?' His tone was consoling. Coping with this situation all by himself had made him come to terms with it fast.

Wiping my tears, I promised not to cry.

'When can we meet Arjun Bhaiya?' I asked.

'Tomorrow, we're going to Tihar to meet him. I've set up an appointment with the lawyer next week.' Then he said, gingerly, eyes shifting restlessly and hands fidgeting, 'Rhea, this is all new and challenging, especially since we're in this soup alone. Papa's sick and Mom's as good as sick. I know I haven't been what one would call 'ideal' and I'm sorry about that. I haven't been a great brother to Arjun either. But I don't want to live with this scare all my life. We need to stick together in this. I can get a little demanding sometimes but try to bear with me.'

I had just promised not to cry, but I couldn't stop a tear from rolling down! I was overwhelmed with emotion. I couldn't believe that Daksh was actually communicating. I wanted to hug him. Tight.

'Daksh, I...' I was at a loss for words. My delight was indescribable.

'Okay, enough of the emotional shit. Don't embarrass me now,' he said, clearly out of his depth and then with a straight-face added, 'Let's get to the point now. We will not talk about any of this business in front of Chacha-Chachi for obvious reasons. Their mouths just happen to open at the wrong moments and to the wrong people all the time. And we have to keep quiet about it in front of Mom too.'

He told me that Arjun Bhaiya's situation was a political issue. His bail plea had been rejected. Arjun was just a pawn; the People's Party and Akul Nair were the actual targets.

'I don't get it, why would they go after Bhaiya of all people?' I questioned.

'It is all very obvious. Arjun had become one of Akul's most important men. You have been away for longer than you think,' he said, looking at the confused frown on my face. 'Akul didn't attend a single public meeting without Arjun. This other jackass, Rajaji, the Hindustan Party's vice-president, wants to protect himself since he's running for elections in the next term. But that will only be possible if all his corruption and malpractices as Minister of New and Renewable Energy are kept under wraps. Unfortunately, our beloved brother and his team have exposed him. Rajaji's only alternative is to prove that those who have accused him are the bad guys. And this is what he is doing. Take a look at these.'

Daksh handed me last week's newspapers. "Stephanian accused of Police Constable's murder'; 'People's Party demonstration takes a violent turn'; 'Nair's right-hand, a murderer?' The lead stories of each newspaper, from *Dainik Jagran* to *Hindustan Times* and the *Times of India*, were all talking about the escapades of Arjun Bedi, a dynamic People's Party member and praiseworthy student of St. Stephen's College, who showed his 'true colours' at the recent demonstration at India Gate. Pictures of the riots against the backdrop of the

Amar Jawan Jyoti added to the impact of the articles.

Until now I had been oblivious to the seriousness of the matter. Front page news coverage was nowhere close to what I'd imagined. The *rajma chawal* I had eaten was desperately trying to find its way up my oesophagus.

'Oh my God! And you said everything was under control? You don't call things under control when the most widely-read newspapers in the country write about your brother being a criminal!' I was hyperventilating and enraged that Daksh had lied to me about this matter. Not once had he mentioned the front page coverage, or any kind of coverage for that matter on Bhaiya!

'Okay, what did you want me to tell you while you were in Yale? That Arjun has been proclaimed a criminal, a ruthless, cold-blooded murderer by the entire nation? That would certainly have made things easier for you there, right? And, knowing this, what could you have done about it? Do you know that I've been hiding these newspapers from Mom? She read one article and developed high fever out of anxiety.' His eyes were bloodshot. My lips trembled. I never meant him to lose his temper like this. I was wrought with guilt. Daksh was already doing a lot and I was getting angry with him for no valid reason.

'I… I'm sorry. I never meant to… ' I stuttered contritely.

'No, I'm sorry. I shouldn't have exploded like that. All this pressure is driving me crazy. And perhaps I should have told you,' Daksh apologised.

I brushed off the matter with a wan smile and got back to the point, 'So the police are also involved, you say?'

'Exactly! That is why his bail plea was overruled. The commissioner, D.P. Singh, has taken the issue into his own hands.'

'But now, what will be our plan of action?' If the police was also involved, there was very little we could do.

'The post-mortem report of Harilal Mathur will be out soon.'

'Then that will disprove all these ludicrous allegations and he'll be released!' I said excitedly. A wave of relief washed over me. I saw a slight sliver of light at the end of the tunnel. But something in Daksh's troubled expression hinted that the matter would perhaps not be sorted out so easily.

'Hopefully that's the turn it will take, otherwise…' Daksh rubbed his chin with his, elegant, artistic fingers. His forehead creased in a frown.

'What otherwise? The post-mortem report will exonerate Bhaiya, won't it?' I questioned worriedly. I did not want to think of any other alternative.

'It should,' he quickly replied. 'Let's forget about this business for a while. Tell me about Yale? How is that chap of yours, what's his name? Abhimanyu.'

I hadn't thought about Abhimanyu since I'd left Yale. He had been more than willing to drop me off at the airport, but Seema Masi and Ajay Masa had come from Pennsylvania to give me moral support while sending me off. Suddenly, thinking about Abhimanyu made my heart ache. In just a few days, I had grown very attached to him. He had been my Rock of Gibraltar in the last week of distress. Now I missed him and his gummy bears! But how did Daksh of all people know about Abhimanyu? I hadn't mentioned him to anyone at home as far as I remembered. Okay, maybe once to Arjun Bhaiya. Not too much, just that I'd finally met someone from India at Yale, and because I thought Bhaiya would be intrigued to know that there was someone who was not overly in love with his place of origin. But I had barely touched upon him. And Arjun Bhaiya would never disclose a secret. Not that this was one…

'What about Abhimanyu? And how do you know about him at all?' I asked, my eyes wide with surprise. Daksh just smirked slyly and quipped, 'I know way more than I let on.'

This was the old Daksh talking again. But the suppressed chuckle assured me that there was nothing more he knew.

'Yeah, yeah. You're the only omniscient one here no?' I provoked him. 'And this reminds me that I have to message him that I've reached home safe and sound.'

'Oh so we've reached the level of checking up on one another, huh?' he teased me.

'Ugh. Shut up! There is nothing like that at all. Can we please change the subject?' I had turned red with embarrassment. I couldn't talk to Daksh about these things!

The next morning Daksh and I went to meet Bhaiya in Tihar Jail. I had heard about the politicians and terrorists and big criminals imprisoned there; I never thought I'd be paying a visit to that place.

Tihar was a parallel world. The conditions were deplorable. At the reception sat Inspector Khare, a young man of no more than thirty. His well-groomed, thick moustache and creaseless uniform spoke of his serious nature. Unlike the stereotypical police officers who were uncouth country bumpkins, Inspector Khare seemed refined and courteous. He directed us to a havildar who guided us inside.

I bit nervously on my lower lip as we walked down the corridors of Tihar. The prisoners shot us dirty glances. I felt extremely awkward and tried to hide behind Daksh. The havildar led us to cell number 8 and opened the lock with a large iron key. Arjun Bhaiya had been imprisoned in a single cell. He sat in a dark corner of the 10×10-foot room, hiding from the narrow beam of sunlight peering in through the microscopic window. His legs were crossed and his head rested on his arms, but when he heard the lock click open, he immediately looked up. He was wearing the blue-and-white striped uniform that all prisoners wore, and looked dejected. His body was lethargic and slow, but his eyes were alert. They were searching for something, someone. Then they alighted on Daksh.

'Daksh,' he said in a voice devoid of any energy. I took a step to the right from behind him, revealing my presence. He leapt to his feet instantaneously and in two quick strides, hugged me warmly. He flinched a little in pain as I hugged him back.

'Bhaiya!'

Daksh nudged me slightly to keep myself under control. We couldn't let Arjun Bhaiya see us in a vulnerable state. We were all that he had, and if we broke down, his courage would be lost and hopes shattered.

'You've become famous, huh?' I said with a wink trying hard to stop my tears and control the tremor in my voice.

Arjun Bhaiya smiled, 'I always told you I would be famous someday.'

The sadness in his voice was apparent although he made an effort to sound confident and cheerful.

'You have half an hour only,' the havildar said and stomped away.

'How are you Bhaiya?' I asked solemnly. The last few days had been hell for him. The fresh gashes on his bare arms sent chills down my back. His knuckles stuck out like an old man's; his skin was crinkled and dry. The deep cut on his forehead seemed to have been made with a knife.

'I've been great. Although I hate this ugly uniform they make us wear here!' he chuckled.

I tried to smile despite the pain I felt when I looked at Arjun Bhaiya. I could never have pictured him like that.

'Arjun Bhaiya,' I said in a serious tone, 'We don't have much time, you know that. And you know the main purpose of our visit here.'

'She's right, it's best if we act quickly,' Daksh said sincerely. I had never heard him talk to Bhaiya with so much humility and respect.

'You guys have to stop acting like some serious surgery has to be performed on me,' Arjun Bhaiya said, trying to lighten the mood. But when he saw that his humour failed to make either of us laugh, he quit trying to ease the atmosphere.

'Okay. Do you think I've actually killed anyone?' he asked in a tone that could only be described as hurting.

'Bhaiya! Why do you think we've come here? To save you. Because we know you haven't done anything at all,' I said. My voice was strong. I believed in Bhaiya. I knew for myself that he was innocent. 'But you have to tell us the sequence of events that day.'

'Arjun, I've set up a meeting with Mr. Kothari, the family lawyer, for next Wednesday. And we need to know your side of the story before that,' Daksh said patiently.

The People's Party, presided over by Akul Nair, had organised one of their biggest protests as a part of their anti-corruption drive at India Gate. It had been organized legitimately, and an estimated figure of the group had been given in advance to the police. Gathering a crowd from Delhi University was one of Arjun Bhaiya's tasks among many others. As Arjun Bhaiya was very popular in college, a large number of Stephanians had already begun to engage in such social movements. Speeches were to be delivered, and social media campaigns to encourage widespread participation were to be initiated. An important part of the agenda was to disclose the 'List of Corrupt' which included names and details of all politicians and bureaucrats who had been involved in scams. The creative head behind the idea was Arjun Bhaiya. The threat of having their grey masks unveiled in front of the public was too grave a risk for these notables to take, especially before the election period. The political leaders featured on the list had already been given an ultimatum by the People's Party to surrender themselves.

On the day of the rally, thousands of people came in groups with their flags and slogans aloft. Men, women, girls and boys— all age groups were present. The aggressive, provocative speeches caused considerable uproar amongst the crowd, and some over-excited demonstrators attempted to break through the security barricades to march towards the presidential palace. Their sudden move ignited a violent turn of events as the police intervened swiftly, as if an unexpected order had been given to them. The crowds were blasted with water cannons. Drenched with water and filled with rage, the people grew more and more agitated and started retaliating. The police now released tear gas on the public, adding to their frustration and anger. To control the infuriated crowd, the police charged with lathis as a last resort. Mayhem spread and riots broke out. Numerous protesters and police officers were severely injured. In this bedlam, a man collapsed. The next thing one knew was that a young student named Arjun Bedi had been arrested for beating and causing the death of Constable Harilal Mathur.

'Daksh, Rhea, not once did I pick up a lathi or even a stone for that matter! Akul Sir had to be escorted back. Just as I was getting to him, a hand tugged at my shirt from amidst the crowd. Suddenly my arms were forced behind my back and a cold, steely snake wrapped itself around my wrists. It was then that I saw a policeman who was chasing the crowd fall flat to the ground.' Arjun Bhaiya sounded wounded and shocked by the sheer outrageousness of the accusation. He still hadn't been able to reconcile himself to what had taken place. This murder allegation had broken him. It had pricked each part of his body, crippling and eventually leaving him completely battered. He was bruised mentally and emotionally, his spirit wilted, as he tried to overcome the shock and disbelief.

'The forensic reports will be out soon,' Daksh said, trying to pacify Arjun Bhaiya. It was obvious his tone from that this was probably not the most helpful of information.

'And we will have Mr. Kothari develop our case. There will be others like you who saw him fall on his own too. We will have witnesses and the reports. There won't be much to worry about,' I exclaimed. The witnesses, the post-mortem report and Mr. Kothari were our weapons in this fight for justice. The goal didn't seem so distant anymore. Arjun Bhaiya's face relaxed momentarily, before he looked worried again.

'What do the daily newspapers say? Must be an embarrassment for you all.'

'No cause for alarm,' Daksh replied with false bonhomie, so contrary to his normally candid nature. I was reminded of T.S Eliot's *Love Song of J. Alfred Prufrock* where in he had written, 'We put on a masque to meet the other masques of the world.'

How very true! Here we were putting on an act to give solace to a hapless brother, an innocent victim of circumstances and political treachery.

'Moreover, everyone knows that you've been implicated,' I added, not wanting to agonise him further.

Arjun Bhaiya smiled. Although he didn't seem to actually believe what I said, a glimmer of hope had been kindled in him.

'There is one thing I don't understand Bhaiya, Akul Nair is such an influential man and you were so important to him. How come he hasn't been able to bail you out?'

Arjun Bhaiya bit on his lip in agitation.

'Because the public would see how the common men of the People's Party are being targeted by big players. D.P. Singh, the commissioner, who is Rajaji's son-in-law, is the culprit behind the police intervention during the protest and getting you arrested. Bail cannot be granted under his reign,' Daksh said firmly, 'At each interview, Akul Nair refutes all criminal charges against you, seeking public sympathy and pity. He tries to show that in front of Rajaji and his powerful connections, particularly Singh, there's very little one can do.'

'Rajaji is behind this? Wait... how do you know all this Daksh?' Arjun Bhaiya was flabbergasted. His eyes looked as if they were going to pop out of their sockets, his flared nose capable of accommodating a whole family of bees.

Daksh flushed.

'I've done my homework over the past few days,' he said, trying to act nonchalant.

'You visited Nair?' Arjun Bhaiya asked.

'Yeah, I met Nair. He gave me the inside story. Rajaji is a very strong man. He'll do everything he can to put People's

Party down. Moreover, he has seen to it that the forensic reports are delayed.'

Arjun Bhaiya shook his head in disgust and disapproval.

'Don't underestimate Rajaji; he is the most tainted and dishonest man I have ever come across. That guy has not earned a single penny through legitimate means. If you look at his accounts, you'll see a flawless record of generating black money,' Arjun Bhaiya said. He now understood how he happened to be in this predicament. The jigsaw puzzle was complete. It all made sense.

We heard the sound of footsteps approaching. It was the havildar telling us that half-an-hour had passed and it was time to leave. I hugged Bhaiya and promised to return with his favourite *boondi ke laddoo* the next day. Daksh held out his hand formally to Bhaiya. But Arjun Bhaiya simply pulled him close and squeezed him tight.

'I love you too, Daksh.'

My eyes were glistening with tears of joy. These two had finally learnt to be brothers again.

As we were leaving, Bhaiya asked rather worriedly, 'How are Mamma and Papa taking all this? They haven't come to see me as yet.'

Before I could even say a word, Daksh answered hurriedly, 'They're fine. Obviously a little anxious about the state of affairs, but they're good. In fact, I've been telling them not to come. Tihar is a scary place. I don't want them to worry more than they need to. Plus Sonu Chacha and Bittu Chachi are here. They keep Mom and Dad very well occupied. Their persistence never fails to impress me! Anyway, you take care; we'll make a move now. Bye.'

His words were abrupt. Arjun Bhaiya was not aware of Papa's coma and Mamma's state.

He would be devastated if he knew and would blame it all on himself. Daksh was right in keeping it from him. Sometimes it is better not to know the truth; sometimes ignorance is bliss.

❧

We went straight to AIIMS from Tihar. Mamma had left for the hospital early in the morning. The whiteness of AIIMS did something to my gut. This was the first time I had been to a hospital—no one in our family had been this ill before. The smell of disinfectant was overpowering, reminding me of my dentist.

'Mr. Param Bedi. Room F-54. I'm his son and this is my sister,' Daksh spoke to the lady at the reception.

'Here are two visitors' passes for you, sir.'

The room was on the first floor. We passed wheelchairs and beds with ailing patients, drips and starched white, uniformed nurses, other visitors with worried faces and doctors clad in lab coats with stethoscopes for necklaces.

We entered room F-54 to see Mamma talking to a slumbering Papa.

'How can you sleep so much? You need to wake up now. Arjun will be out of jail soon. The post-mortem reports of that constable will be out and they'll know that he wasn't murdered by our son. Rhea's also back from Yale. She got back last night. She looks happy and confident, you know. It was a very good decision to have sent her there. Arjun is so far-sighted. I'm going to send him some food soon. Maybe *puri-alloo*. You also like that don't you? I won't have to cook two times then.' She giggled. 'I'm just kidding; I'll cook as many times as you want me to cook, anything that you want me to cook. Remember, you told me you liked eating the food that I cooked and not Kashi's? I've started cooking a lot now. Kashi has almost no work. You need to come back home now.' Something suddenly came over her; she went hysterical and started screaming, 'Param! Wake up now! Look I've cooked for you! Wake up!' then with defeated helplessness and tears rolling down her cheeks she pleaded, 'Please wake up, just please...' and sat on the floor in despair.

I stopped as if struck. I was numb and my heart had stopped beating. There was no way I could remain in there. This was my own mother. Talking to my unresponsive father. In no time, Daksh had taken two long strides and was holding Mamma in his arms. He was whispering something in her ear and she was nodding. Supporting her, he led her to the sofa and made her sit down. Daksh gave me an earnest look.

'Let me call Dr. Jai, okay?' he told Mamma and walked to the door to ask a nurse to send for Dr. Jai Verma, the neuro-physician. Then he came to stand by my side as we both gazed silently at Mamma.

'It is very difficult for her. She comes here every day with the hope that Dad will wake up. He will, soon, but everything takes time. She just needs to be told that constantly. And you don't have to remain here if you don't want to. It can be depressing to see your mother in hysterics and father lying like a vegetable,' Daksh said to me, his face filled with understanding and concern.

I blinked away my tears and simply nodded.

'I'll wait outside, please?' I asked.

'Yeah. It won't take too long.'

I watched Dr. Jai walk into the room. He walked out with Daksh a few minutes later. Daksh shook hands with him and then re-entered the room to emerge after sometime.

'The doctor says he is stable and we shouldn't worry about him. He is responding to all the medicines satisfactorily. So that is some good news. I've told mom that we'll be leaving now, she'll come back in the evening sometime.'

'Yeah okay,' I said quietly. I wanted to get back home, anywhere out of this dismal place.

The time change; the exertion of travel; the depressing atmosphere at home; the alarming condition of Papa, overwhelmed with all these problems, I had no time to attend to the demands of my body. Now benumbed with angst, I needed some respite to face life better. But much to my displeasure, when I rang the doorbell, a loud, uncouth voice screamed out in a Punjabi accent, 'Comeeeeeing *ji!*'

Decked up in a red-and-gold suit that only heightened her chubbiness, her forehead adorned with a big *bindi*, Bittu Chachi opened the door, looking like a bride.

'*Putta*r Rhea!' she cried out loudly and clutched me tightly to her bosom.

When I bowed down to touch her feet in respect I saw Daksh simply ignoring her and walking inside without an acknowledgement. Chachi made a face at him and mumbled something to herself.

In a mixture of broken English, Hindi and Punjabi, she asked me how I was and about my experiences at Yale. Then with fake sympathy and concern she asked, 'Arjun *ka kya hal? Jail mein hi hai?*' (What has happened to Arjun, is he still in jail?)

I really did not want to waste my time talking to Chachi and answering her idiotic and deliberately upsetting questions, so I nodded and told her I was very tired and going to bed.

The following morning's *Hindustan Times* declared: 'Reports of People's Case soon to be out'. Daksh and I went through the whole article more than a hundred times, but there was no mention of exactly when the result would be out. In a state of dire ambiguity and doubt we decided to call Tihar Jail for information.

The phone rang, but no one answered the first time. We called again, and this time a deep voice answered. Daksh spoke.

'Hello, I'm Daksh Bedi, brother of Arjun Bedi,' he paused, 'prisoner number 234, cell number 8. Who is on line?'

'Hello, Mr. Bedi. This is Inspector Khare. How can I help you?'

'Inspector Khare, I read in the newspaper today that the report of the post-mortem would be out soon. I would like to know exactly when it will be out.'

'Um, Mr. Bedi, I'm afraid that information cannot be divulged yet. The media will obviously be kept in the loop, so the news will reach you the moment the report is out.'

'Inspector Khare,' Daksh's tone became stiff and hard, 'I don't think you understand. This is my brother that we're talking about. His case needs to be attended to by a lawyer and that can only happen if we get the facts right. I need to know when the report will be out.'

'Mr. Bedi, I know it is a serious matter. I've seen you visit your brother several times; and yesterday you came here with your sister. I would like to help you in whatever way I can, but the reports are confidential right now. Even I don't know what's in them.'

Daksh's temper was rising, but he tried to keep a firm hold on his anger. 'Inspector, do you even understand the gravity of the matter? As a citizen of the Democratic Republic of India, it is my right to know. So please do the needful.'

'I will get back to you with whatever information I can, please don't worry. As a servant of the Republic of India, I will do all I can to serve you.'

'Thank you Inspector. I will personally come to visit you this evening.'

Daksh wasn't particularly thrilled with the result of the conversation, but there wasn't much he could do on the phone.

Chachi came into the living-room. When she read the headlines, she shrieked, in Punjabi of course, 'Oh, what hell has broken out on the family! Because of Arjun, the name of the entire family has gone to the dogs! God save us, please save us!'

We all knew annoying Daksh was like lighting a match to a gas cylinder. He took less than a few seconds to explode.

'Chachi, shut up. Kindly go back inside and do not interfere in our personal matters. You're older than me so I have to treat you with respect, but don't cross your limits or I may do so too,' Daksh's tone was steely but controlled.

Bittu Chachi was dumbstruck; but what could she have said anyway? She muttered something about parents, manners and courtesy before leaving the room in a huff.

Turning to me as though nothing had occurred, Daksh asked, 'Rhea, you know where Mom keeps the keys to her cupboard, right?'

He asked me to get a bundle of 1,000-rupee notes from a white plastic packet. It was a thick bundle. It's strange how drastically life changes. One moment you're sitting in the passenger seat of a car with your seatbelt safely secured. A small speed bump or two doesn't make much of a difference because you know the airbags will save you. Besides you trust the driver, who is steering you. And then, a colossal jolt and you're thrown diving into the driver's seat, no seatbelt or airbags. The speed breakers that come now are those that give you big judders. Nothing can save you now from being flung on to the road. It is up to you to cross these hurdles and find your way. And in the course of doing so there are tiny pebbles, like Chacha and Chachi, that you must dodge.

Daksh called Mr. Kothari and confirmed our appointment with him for Wednesday. Then we drove all the way to Tihar Jail. But this time it was mainly to meet Inspector Khare. He was at the reception desk going through what seemed like case files.

'Inspector Khare,' Daksh called out to him, extending his hand.

'Mr Daksh Bedi. You're here,' he said and gave me a polite nod of acknowledgement.

Daksh wasn't the kind to beat about the bush; he got straight to the point.

'Any information about the reports?'

'Mr Bedi, I must say you're quite an adamant young man. The reports should be out by tonight.'

Daksh said, 'Mister, I don't know if you know how very important this is to us. My father is in coma. My mother is on anti-depressants; we need to save our brother. We really do.'

Inspector Khare smiled sympathetically and said, 'Daksh, you're a very young boy. In the course of my job, I have interacted with a lot of prisoners, all of whom have been, how to put it, not very cooperative. Your brother, on the other hand, he has never once acted up or misbehaved. When we study crime, a very important aspect of it is also criminal psychology. I know what comprises a criminal. Your brother doesn't fit into that category. The moment the reports are out, you will be the first to know. As I said before, I will do all I can to help.' He was earnest. His sincerity made me trust him despite my prejudice against policemen.

We went and met Arjun Bhaiya after that. He devoured the *boondi ke laddoo*, savouring each morsel. As the clock ticked, our anxiety increased. At least Daksh's and mine did. Weirdly, it was Arjun Bhaiya who was trying to calm us. He seemed so much in control of his emotions.

'Rhea, Daksh, you guys really need to chill. The reports will be out soon. Things will get back to normal again. One must have faith in God and in truth. Everything will be fine.'

After the 'Mulakat' time was over, Daksh and I said goodbye to Bhaiya and Inspector Khare. He had taken Daksh's number to inform us the moment the reports were out. We drove home without a word. Tension was building up with each passing second. Rajaji was a corrupt, dishonest man. Plus, he was a man with power and influence. We were just a little unsure about the extent of his influence. The TV was blaring out from Chacha and Chachi's room. Sensitivity was obviously not their strong point. Despite knowing what the situation at home was like, they still didn't seem to care.

It was ten-thirty at night when Daksh's mobile rang. Mamma had come back home and retired to bed, although I doubted if she was actually sleeping.

I hurried to view the caller; it was a landline number. I answered it quickly.

'Hello? Is this Daksh Bedi?' The voice was Inspector Khare's. A cold current went through me. I felt giddy.

'It's Rhea, Inspector. The reports are out?' I was afraid to know the answer to the question I had just asked.

'Hello, Rhea. Yes they are. If it isn't too late, do you think you and your brother could make a trip here? It would be better to talk in person.' There was something in his voice that told me that the news wasn't very pleasant.

'If you could just hold on Inspector, I'll call my brother.'

I passed the phone to Daksh. He didn't say anything, just nodded and in the end said, 'I'll be there in fifteen minutes,' and hung up.

'Daksh? What did he tell you?' I asked curiously.

'Nothing much Rhea. I'm going to go meet Khare, you stay at home, take care of Mom.' Daksh didn't look at me in the eye. He kept fiddling with his phone and tying his shoelaces over and over again.

'What do you mean I? We are going. You stay at home if you want to take care of Mamma,' I said crossly. How could he suddenly cut me out like that?

'Don't be silly, Rhea.'

'Daksh you need to know, once and for all, that we are in this together. And I think you were the one who said that in the first place? If you're going to meet Khare then you jolly well know that I'm going along with you too.' Obstinacy was one thing Daksh and I had in common. He knew I wouldn't budge from my decision. At all.

It was raining outside. There were flashes of lightning and loud claps of thunder, a scene worthy of a Shakespearean tragedy, where the forces of nature were like a foreboding of things to come. The only difference was that this wasn't Shakespeare or Milton, it was reality. Ugh. I had to stop thinking like this.

We didn't go to Tihar. Daksh parked the car in front of Café Rodeo in Connaught Place.

'Why're we here?' I asked. I thought we had to meet Khare in Tihar.

'He'll meet us in here.' Daksh was terse. He was never much of a conversationalist anyway, and now his voice was much more curt than usual. Something was definitely not right. I felt giddy again.

We ordered coffee in Rodeo and waited for Khare. A young man with a thick, black moustache walked in. His gait was confident. When he sat down in front of us, I realized that it was Inspector Khare. He was quite a hunk out of his uniform!

'Rhea, Daksh. Good evening,' he said.

When Daksh didn't respond, I said, 'Hello.'

'What about the autopsy?' Daksh asked.

'That's why I'm here,' Khare said. 'The reports state that Constable Harilal Mathur died of brain haemorrhage that was caused by external force.'

'What?' I asked, stupefied.

'You two need to listen carefully now. The post-mortem reports are not in your favour. The prosecution will make its case fast, now it has concrete evidence. Find yourselves a good lawyer. I heard on the grapevine that Commissioner D.P. Singh is taking charge of the case. This piece of information will spread in no time at all. You need to fight. You need to fight hard. And you need to fight fast.'

'Rhea, we have to meet Kothari tomorrow,' Daksh said to me.

Inspector Khare couldn't have been more right about the news spreading. As we were driving back home with heavy hearts, I got a call from Jayshree Masi asking me to watch the Aaj Tak news. The topic of discussion was the Stephanian murder case!

We reached home and immediately turned on the TV and heard a news journalist read out,

'The post-mortem reports of Harilal Mathur, the police constable who was a victim of the brutal riots at the recent People's Party demonstration at India Gate, are out now. The reports which were earlier made confidential by Commissioner D.P. Singh due to security purposes are now publicly viewable. The reports show that Constable Harilal Mathur died of a brain haemorrhage caused by an external blow to the head. The police claims of Mathur being pitilessly beaten up by Delhi-based Arjun Bedi, an active member of the People's Party, have been proven correct. Mathur, who was trying to control the crowds, was heartlessly trampled and assaulted by the young Stephanian who also happened to be one of the chief forces behind the campaign.'

I was paralysed by what I had just heard; I didn't know what to think, of whom to think or what to do. I was completely devoid of any feeling. Allegations and accusations were one thing, but they had explicitly called my brother a murderer. Abhimanyu was right; in a country like ours, fairness is a concept that is applicable in sports and suchlike, it doesn't exist in real-life situations. The common man has no place here. The truth gets buried and the innocent are penalized for crimes they have not committed. That's the irony of Indian life. We just turn a blind eye to injustice and exploitation by our lackadaisical, apathetic attitudes, living in a make-believe world of 'Incredible India', loftily claiming *Saare Jahan Se Accha*. Now I could relate to Abhimanyu and understand the abhorrence he had for a country where corruption is truly prevalent, creeping intrinsically into the very fabric of Indian life, where innocent people are sent to gallows, where selfish politicans with vested interests exercise power and authority with their crafty mechanisations.

I looked at Daksh, hoping to find some solace in him. As he stared into the TV screen, I saw his eyes glisten in the reflection of the light. It was the first time I had ever seen Daksh in such a state. Daksh was the aloof, detached kind. Today, he was breaking down.

'We're meeting Kothari tomorrow Daksh,' I said slowly, trying to reassure him, but my words sounded hollow.

'Yes. Yes we are,' he said and got up from the sofa, his body taut, fists tightly clenched. Walking slowly, he went into his room without saying another word. I didn't follow him; I knew he needed to be alone. I did too.

I had never felt so helpless. It hurt me to think about Arjun Bhaiya—in the prison uniform he found so ugly, his unrestrained laughter—and do nothing to save him. I wanted someone to comfort me, to be by my side and tell me that all would be fine. But as I looked behind me, an empty wall gaped back mockingly.

❦

Mr. Kothari's office was posh and luxuriously decorated. We waited for over an hour at the reception. Daksh was getting visibly impatient. He kept skimming through the same pages of the *Stardust* magazine and mumbling to himself. Finally the receptionist ushered us in. Mr. Kothari, who had sounded so eager and enthusiastic on the phone the previous day, now looked as if all his zeal and fervour had petered out. He busied himself with a pile of papers on his table as we waited for him to acknowledge us.

'Yes, Daksh Bedi?' he asked, almost indifferently. He knew the entire story. Daksh had related it to him in detail, yet he was asking. Daksh was already annoyed and I knew it wouldn't take him much time to explode so I decided to do the talking.

'Hello. I'm Rhea. We need your help, sir. Daksh has already given you the main facts yesterday. Our brother has been implicated in a murder case,' I said.

'Yes. I'm quite aware of the whole case. It's the hottest topic on all the news channels. The autopsy reports are out, I'm sure you both know about that now.'

'Of course we do,' Daksh spoke with his teeth clenched. His face contorted, but he made a desperate effort to maintain a calm façade.

'So you must also know what they show, that Harilal Mathur died of a brain haemorrhage. Daksh, Rhea, I know you are very concerned about your brother and you believe in him. But there are times in our lives when our Hyde takes over our Jekyll and that innate evil surfaces.'

I couldn't believe my ears. Had this Kothari actually said what I thought he had? A knot developed in my gut. I saw Daksh's hands quiver.

'What are you trying to imply, Mr. Kothari?' I asked.

'No matter how much I may want to believe in the fact that your brother is innocent, I can't. The facts speak differently.' There was no compassion in his voice. He seemed to be having fun instead.

Daksh was just going to say something when I touched his arm, indicating that he stay calm and composed.

'Mr. Kothari, I've come to you to help me out of this soup.

Instead, you are accusing my brother of being a murderer. I'm your client, Mr. Kothari.' My voice was firm, despite my inner turmoil.

'Rhea, I'm sorry but I can't take your case,' Mr. Kothari said curtly. His face was impassive.

'Mr. Kothari, we need you, you are our last ray of hope,' I pleaded. Then I said very sincerely, trying to stop the tears from forming in my eyes, 'Mr. Kothari, I'm just seventeen and Daksh is eighteen. Our dad is in coma. Our mom is so consumed with stress that she is in a world of her own. We don't have anyone to go to Mr. Kothari. We are desperate. Please accept our case. I know my brother is innocent. Just please, please help us out. I… I beg of you.'

'The reports say something else Rhea. And I have a reputation to maintain. I'm sorry, I can't help you.'

'Fine' said Daksh.

I was taken aback. What was Daksh doing? I tried to reason with him but he cut me off.

'It's fine Rhea, we don't need to fall at anyone's feet. He can have his own opinion. He can think and do as he likes. If he wants to go lick that Rajaji's ass, he can jolly well do that.' He said all this looking straight into Kothari's eyes. The fire that burnt in Daksh could easily have burnt Kothari in that instant. Rather it was already burning him.

Mr. Kothari turned purple.

'Boy, stay within your limits!' He shouted.

'Tell me where I'm wrong, sir?' Daksh smirked, his eyes still looking piercingly at Mr. Kothari.

'There are legal obligations that I have to abide by,' he said in a quieter tone.

'Don't try to fool yourself sir. What obligations they are, I know only too well.'

And then turning to me he said, 'Let's make a move Rhea. There is no time to waste with assholes.' He got up instantly, with me following close behind.

Mr. Kothari was scandalized. His face was drained of all colour. There wasn't a single word he could say. His phone rang. The ringtone was the iconic Grande Valse, the typical Nokia tone. 'Rajaji,' the automated name-caller spoke aloud in an American accent.

'Yeah, tell him his work's done,' Daksh added with a malicious smile.

'Daksh, I have political commitments. Even if I may want to help, I can't. My hands are tied. I-'

And Daksh banged the door shut. Kothari was a bundle of contradictions. There was no point in wasting time with such an undependable and unreliable person.

We got into the car and immediately Daksh's confident and assertive mask crumpled.

'Daksh! What was that over there? Are you stupid? It wasn't the time to get angry and throw your tantrums! Where are we going to get a lawyer from? What are we going to do at all!' I screamed at Daksh. What he did was highly irresponsible and impetuous. Kothari was the only anchor we could hold on to, but now all hope was lost.

I was caught up in a whirlpool of emotions—seething anger, frustration and helplessness while my bantering was met with sad silence.

THE BIRTH OF HOPE

It was two am. Daksh and I were sitting in the living room watching the news flashes about Arjun Bhaiya when the bell rang. Who could it be at this hour of the night? I got up and walked silently to the door. I put my eye against the peephole and saw the silhouette of a tall man standing alone in the moonlight. A man at the door at this time of the night? I was suspicious. A kidnapper, or maybe one of Rajaji's hitmen, I thought to myself.

'Dear God, save me,' I muttered under my breath, my heart beating faster.

I motioned to Daksh as streaks of lightning filled the sky, illuminating the clouds with an ominous yellow glow. The thunderbolt that followed shook me. Another loud clap of thunder made the paintings on the walls shake, petrifying me further. My heart was hammering in my chest, as I grabbed the nearest thing I could find to defend myself—a coffee-table book on photography.

'Great,' I muttered, tossing it aside. A book could hardly save me if I was up against the cold steel of a gun or the sharp edge of a knife. Daksh gestured me to stay where I was and left the room. He returned a few seconds later, holding a sturdy cricket bat. Without further ado, I flung open the door and Daksh charged outside, straight at the intruder.

The silhouette's scream deafened my ears.

'What the hell is wrong with you?' he shouted while Daksh thrashed him. 'Stop it!'

'Who the hell are you, freaking beast!' I shrieked, loud enough to wake the neighbours.

'Rhea! It's me, Abhimanyu! And you fool, stop hitting me!'

I wasn't sure if I had heard the right name. Did the man say he was Abhimanyu? Daksh stopped his martial arts to turn on the porch lights.

'Who is this Rhea?' He stared hard at the man. His chest was heaving with rage.

The man's eyes were tight with pain. This was the face that used to haunt my dreams.

'Abhimanyu,' I said, but it came out like a sigh. Suddenly all the pent-up pain and stress of the past days burst forth like water released from a dam.

'Hello, young man? We run on Indian time in New Delhi; it's not New Haven,' Daksh spoke furiously.

'Yeah, buddy. I'm sorry about that,' Abhimanyu replied sheepishly. 'I just wanted to-'

'And could you just barge in like this into anyone's house in the middle of the night? And that too without informing them? You can pull that off there, but not here. People actually sleep at this hour. Wait, Rhea did you know about this?' Daksh directed his last question toward me. He was starting to feel the effects of the entire day's stress and strain. But though he probably believed that I had known of Abhimanyu's programme, I did not. I was equally flabbergasted to see him at my doorstep. It would have been better had I known; at least I wouldn't have welcomed him wearing an ugly teddy bear nightsuit!

'I had no idea at all.' I was still in a trance. I'd often pictured Abhimanyu coming back to India, but I was sure that it was only the stuff that dreams are made of.

'I'm sorry; I didn't mean to bother you guys like this. It was a sudden decision, I didn't think,' Abhimanyu said apologetically.

'Abhimanyu! Are you silly? I'm so happy you're here. Come inside, the weather is horrid anyway,' I said excitedly.

He looked apprehensively at Daksh, as if seeking his permission. Daksh gave him a stern look, staring straight into his eyes before nodding reluctantly. He stomped into his room after telling me, 'You're handling Chachi,' with a nod in Abhimanyu's direction.

This may sound like a cliché, but Abhimanyu and I kept gazing into each other's eyes for what seemed like almost a century. There was some magnetic force that had attracted me to him the moment I had met him; that energy was as overpowering even today. He took a step towards me, his eyes, soft and gentle, penetrating deep into my soul. He looked at me as if he knew exactly what I was feeling. I felt awkward, naked and exposed. He wrapped his arms around me. I closed my eyes, comforted by his presence. I smiled, I hadn't felt such happiness for a long time. I didn't want to break away from him, not so soon. No one had given me a cuddle or a word of reassurance since I had come back to Delhi.

'How are things here?' he asked, speaking into my hair.

My blissful bubble burst and I returned to reality.

'Not good, not good at all,' I said mumbling into his chest. He caressed my hair and said very sincerely, 'All will be well now, you don't have to worry. I'll take care of everything.'

After giving him a glass of water, I asked the question that was uppermost in my mind: 'How come you're here? I thought you had pledged never to set foot in India ever again.'

'For you,' he said; his face just inches away from mine.

'But,' he said breaking the mood, 'that does not change my notion of India being a crazy place. Today, after a fourteen-hour flight from JFK to the New Delhi airport, with wailing children and the yucky odour of rancid oil my only company, I landed on Indian soil with a suitcase and a backpack. When I went to the counter to order a taxi, I was informed that taxis would be available after thirty minutes, but I could get one on the road outside the terminus building if I wanted one immediately. I don't understand why you would display a board saying 'Taxis Available' if one had to get them from the road! I don't understand these Indian systems at all!' he cribbed. 'Anyway, I had placed be my suitcase beside me while talking to the official, but when I turned to pick up my bag, I found that it wasn't there. In less than two minutes it had vanished! Just like that, into thin air!' he cursed. 'The airport officials said that "the luggage was not their responsibility once it had been handed to the owner," and therefore no assistance was offered! Had this been the US, they would have checked the cameras and I would have received my bag the very next day with a note of apology and a plate of cookies!'

Abhimanyu's disbelief was apparent. But there was more to his story than his airport experience.

'Finally I made my way to find a taxi to drive me to a hotel. But when I reached the road, two drivers came running up to me, one of them literally snatching the backpack out of my hand and the other almost groping me! All this to get me to sit in their cab. The two men went mad! Thank God I wasn't a girl! Then it would have been sheer harassment,' he proclaimed with contempt. 'But what followed was even more bewildering! Why do you think I came to your place at this hour? I'm not stupid and as a matter of fact, I do know people in India run on IST and not on American time,' he added seriously in response to Daksh's taunt.

'After getting into one of the taxis, I asked the driver to take me to a decent hotel in a central location. The driver was Bengali. With a naughty smile and in as much English as he could manage he said, "Yung bai, fram Amrica? Bhery good bhery good. Want *pataka* at night? Bhery good night you hab."' Abhimanyu mimicked the driver's Bengali accent perfectly! He was just so cute! But I couldn't fall in love at this stage, I told myself sternly.

'I disregarded his question and told him to just take me to the hotel. As we were driving, a speeding BMW rammed into an auto that was on the same side of the road. What was amazing was the fact that the car's driver did not even stop to look at what had happened; he just whizzed past. I told my driver to stop in case any help was required. This led to a volley of excuses—that the police would come, his licence would be cancelled and other shit. It was only after I insisted did he stop. The auto had two passengers—a man and a young boy, probably his son—and of course the driver. Although the driver wasn't hurt, the man seemed to have broken his leg. His son was crying with fright,' Abhimanyu broke off. There was another clap of thunder. I was quite at a loss to understand why a stranger's accident should have such an effect on him.

'Abhimanyu?' I tried bringing him back to this world. 'What happened next?'

'Oh, sorry! Nothing. I took them to the hospital in my taxi. The little boy was petrified. You know how ten-year olds are? He thought his father was going to die.' Abhimanyu tried to laugh but it came out like a forced snort.

'Oh. That's a sad but happy story, I guess?' I said.

'Yeah, I felt good that I helped. Then the taxi driver drove me down to some Cabella Inn. I checked into my room which was, let's put it mildly, slightly unusual, with its shiny red curtains and flowery bedsheets. Although these were just the outward trappings, I hated it there. With my suitcase lost, I didn't even have any clothes. My recent experiences were wearing me down, and I guess I wanted to be somewhere like home. So I came here. I'm sorry.'

'Uh! Shut up!'

Then changing the topic which was getting a little heavy, I said with a giggle, 'You mentioned the driver asking you if you wanted a *pataka*?'

'Oh yeah! That was weird!' He screwed up his face in mock disgust, making me laugh.

'Okay, wouldn't it have been equally funny had I agreed?' he asked, provoking me with a sly grin.

I stopped laughing. The joke was on me now.

'Shut up,' I said curtly. I knew he was kidding but I didn't want such a thought to even cross his mind. I was a little jealous, and maybe a little possessive too, but it wasn't such a bad thing, was it?

'Why, now I think I should have agreed, no?' he teasing me even further.

'Well, too bad that you didn't. I'm going to sleep. You're jetlagged, I'm not anymore. So,' I said getting up from the sofa, 'Bye. Have a good night's sleep, *if* at all you sleep,' with special emphasis on the 'if'.

Things were the same then and they are the same now! The value of life is as little as it was before! People in India want easy access to things; they resort to shortcuts in this journey of life and have no scruples when it comes to taking what they want. Otherwise how can a person walk away so easily after ramming into someone or even filching another's belongings? And that too, unconcerned about the discomfort caused to the unsuspecting victim. They live for themselves—totally oblivious to the inconvenience and the suffering they cause to others. In this selfish scenario, who cares about the woes of the other? What makes them to be so callously selfish, I wonder? Is it avarice or just an easy way out to become rich overnight? It defies my imagination. Such unmindful acts can lead to irreparable damage and have grave repercussions. Why can't people understand the gravity of the situation? The very thought of such unscrupulous acts curdles my blood!

I was touched by Abhimanyu's kind gesture to have come all the way to India just to be by my side. I had put up a strong face in front of him, but inside I was completely broken. For a while, I had put Arjun Bhaiya and Papa out of my mind, but now I was back to reality. I went into my room and saw Daksh sitting quietly by the bed. He had curled himself into a tight ball, and was rocking himself back and forth. He looked defeated. The distressing events of the past week or so had finally taken their toll.

Daksh's anguish devastated me. I placed a reassuring hand on his shoulder which he shrugged off promptly. I got into bed and tried to sleep. But even hours of counting sheep in my head did not distract me from the painful thoughts of Bhaiya's plight. I got up quietly, not wanting to disturb Daksh who was now asleep, and walked outside to check on Abhimanyu. The immense care and affection he had displayed made me extremely sensitive to his needs and I didn't want to hurt or disappoint him in any way. I tiptoed quietly into the living room. The comforter I had given him had fallen to the ground. I picked it up and gingerly spread it over his sleeping body. Abhimanyu was tired after the long flight and the night's adventures. I sat by his side. I wanted to stroke his hair, but didn't. What would he or anyone else think if they saw me do so? Shaking my head in disapproval, I went back to my room to endure a few more hours of sleepless anxiety.

Because of my jetlag, I was up the entire night. My mind was running wild with thoughts of the past, the present and the future. I was suddenly reminded of the "Stream of Consciousness' technique" James Joyce had adopted in Ulysses. *I was troubled by persistent doubts. The ghosts of my past haunted me. Was it a good decision for me to have returned to India? Yes, it was right, my inner voice told me. I heard the soft patter of footsteps. I closed my eyes, not wanting to answer any questions as to why I was awake. A gentle hand picked up the comforter and spread it softly over my body. I opened one eye to observe Rhea walk back to her room. Her kind gesture was enough to sweep me off my feet again. It was certainly a correct decision! Cuddling one of the tiny cushions, I slowly drifted into a deep slumber letting go of my jetlag, my day's fatigue and my anxious thoughts of an unpredictable future.*

I awoke to the sound of Bittu Chachi's screams.

'*Eh ji, sunte ho? Dekho ghar naal kaun aa gaya hai*!' she hollered crudely in Punjabi.

I scuttled outside to see what the matter was. I didn't want to be embarrassed in front of Abhimanyu, but I already was too late. Looking like a little blue elephant in her baby blue salwar-suit, Bittu Chachi was peering down at Abhimanyu as though he was a specimen from another planet.

'Chachi! He is a friend of mine. Stop it!' I said.

'*Ji ki ho gaya si? E kaun hai*?' Sonu Chacha walked in wearing striped boxers with his hair cascading down his shoulders.

'Sonu Chacha, nothing is wrong. This is a friend of mine who has come from the US,' I said trying to shoo everyone away from Abhimanyu.

'Uh, good morning, Uncle,' Abhimanyu said, turning red.

'Boy in the house! What kalyug!' Chachi screamed. 'Parjayiji!' she called out loudly.

'What's happened? What's all this commotion? What's wrong Bittu?' Mom came in looking disturbed.

'Mamma! Calm down! Remember Abhimanyu? From Yale? Well he is here. He came here early this morning only because he didn't have a hotel booking,' I told her.

A white lie. But it was justified.

'Hi beta, how're you doing?' she asked him.

'I'm great, uh, Mrs Bedi. I was just leaving, thank you for having me over,' he said awkwardly.

Mrs Bedi?! Really? I stifled my laugh.

She nodded at him pleasantly and said, 'You must stay for breakfast. Don't go on an empty stomach,' then turned to me with a serious expression and said, 'I'm leaving for the hospital, can you handle everything here?'

I nodded alertly.

If that had been an embarrassing moment, then what followed at the breakfast table was even worse.

'Abhimanyu,' began Chachi, trying to flaunt her powers of speech, 'you fram Amrica?'

'Yeah, I did college there,' he answered briefly.

I dropped my spoon in embarrassment. I didn't dare to say a single word or even look at Abhimanyu. I just kept my fingers crossed hoping that Chachi would stop her interrogation.

'My daughter, Dolly, is very jolly. She want to marry Amrican boy, you know some boy?' she continued. I turned red like a tomato.

'Uh, what?' Abhimanyu asked, clearly amused.

Chachi saw me give her an angry look and quickly said with a laugh, 'Nothingji, I was toh joking, Here take some makkhan on the parantha,' she said, dropping a big dollop of butter on Abhimanyu's parantha.

'No, no! I am on a diet, I don't have butter,' he cried in alarm.

'What diet, so young you are. Butter is good for health,' Bittu Chachi said showing off her flabby biceps.

I explained to Abhimanyu later that though Chachi was irritating, she was a good-natured person who believed in the philosophy of "eat, drink and be merry, for tomorrow we may die". Her insatiable desire to know what's happening in other people's lives is so great that she can't understand why she's not welcome. Nor can she take a hint if you wish to avoid her. Her talents lay in prying into everything and giving unwanted suggestions. She took undue liberties and her exuberant displays of affection were sometimes uncalled for and exasperating.

Looking at Rhea's aunt, I was suddenly reminded of a neighbour back home in Varanasi. Her charm, her benevolence, her way of persuading me to eat paranthas and her overwhelming concern for someone whom she had met for the first time, raked up a memory lying dormant in my mind. Flashback to my neighbour's daughter— the irresistible attraction to the opposite sex, waiting for hours to catch a glimpse of her face—how young and immature I was then! I'll never forget the love letter which she passed on to my mother and the commotion it created at home and the embarrassment I faced in front of them all. I never dared to look or approach that girl again. That experience was humiliation personified for a teenage boy.

MERCHANT OF CHANGE

I knew Abhimanyu had lost his suitcase. Without talking about it, I placed a T-shirt and a pair of pants by his backpack. He had come from such a distance; the least I could do was to be a generous host.

'Abhimanyu, Daksh and I will be leaving for Tihar to meet Bhaiya in a bit. Is there any place you want us to drop you?' I asked after breakfast.

'That would be great. If Akul Nair's office is on the way, maybe you could drop me off there?'

'Oh, you mean the People's Party office?' I asked sceptically.

'Yeah.'

I gave a quick nod and said, 'Just get dressed fast; Daksh hates waiting.'

Why would Abhimanyu want to go to the People's Party office? Those fraudulent hypocrites! Bhaiya had been in jail for so many days and not once had Nair gone to meet him, let alone help with his bail.

'Got that! And, one more thing,' he said, a little shyly. 'Thanks.'

'What for?' I asked, genuinely perplexed.

'Well, the fact that you let me stay here last night, that

you saved me from embarrassment in front of your mom, for the big fat dollop of butter and also for the clothes that you placed by my backpack.'

I smiled and shrugged.

Daksh raised his eyebrows behind Abhimanyu's back and gave an amused smile.

So much had occurred in her life, with her family, and I hadn't spoken to her about it. The perpetual frown lines on Daksh's forehead spoke of his mental agony. It was imperative for me to support Rhea in this moment of crisis. She looked lost, as if standing at a crossroad, not knowing where to turn. I wish to be a pillar of strength for both Rhea and Daksh who seemed damned and doomed. The entire family seems to have reached a saturation point for nothing seems to be working. I want to rejuvenate their sagging spirits and pull them out of this nadir of despair and hopelessness. I want to help in every which way I can. I thought Rohit, my senior at Yale, who had started working with the People's Party would be able to give some details about Arjun's detention. Thus, I decided to visit Akul Nair's office. When I saw that Akul Nair's office was very modest, it came as a bit of a surprise for me. But it was a pleasant surprise. The ordinariness of the headquarters made me believe in the People's Party's cause. They had so much of public support, they ought to be different. I was escorted to the war room from the reception.

From IITians to Chicago-based neonatologists, US-based software engineers, all of them had left their jobs to be a part of the People's Party. They were all there to be a part of a cause, to make politics more ethical. It was heartwarming to hear these intellectuals impart their views; their enthusiasm was inspiring. The People's Party's vision to change the culture of politics in India.

The dirty politics that has been flourishing since independence had to be exterminated and a young, youth-driven India had to come into existence. Bananas and Indian politicians had one thing in common—both should have their skins peeled to feed the monkeys! The common man has been at the mercy of government officials for too long and this dirty system has to end. The zeal and determination for change was very obvious. A wave of optimism swept over me and I felt that something good was actually in the waiting for this country. Hearing those enthused talks, I felt assured that Arjun could be helped. The People's Party's intentions were good; unlike the other political parties whose main aim was to gain authoritarian power, the party target was to uplift the downtrodden and the poverty stricken.

Abhimanyu looked very satisfied after his visit to the People's Party office. He talked of all the great things they envisaged and how this motivated group of people had the potential to revolutionize India. But more than India, he seemed certain that the People's Party would be able to help with Arjun's case. I was reluctant to burst his bubble of optimisim, but I had to tell him what the reality was. After meeting Arjun Bhaiya in Tihar Jail, we had tried to approach Akul Nair many times, but he had provided no help whatsoever. He had been indifferent to our concerns, even though he had always stated that Arjun Bhaiya was his right hand man. Nair talked of many things, but very few actions followed. He was such a chameleon! Such a Brutus, stabbing his Julius like that! The People's Party was using Bhaiya as a scapegoat. It could have taken Nair less than a second to get Arjun Bhaiya out of jail, but he had taken no action whatsoever. It was all for public sympathy and publicity. To portray how the government was accusing innocent men like the members of the People's Party of crimes they had never committed. Abhimanyu listened to me intently, flabbergasted by how two-faced someone could be.

❦

Daksh had helped Abhimanyu find a place to stay. The Jukaso Inn was very close to our house and was also very reasonable. Daksh and I were going to Tihar again the next day. Abhimanyu willingly accompanied us.

On the way to Tihar Jail, Daksh and I briefed Abhimanyu about the entire state of affairs. We told him how Arjun Bhaiya was being implicated on charges of murder, how the autopsy reports had dashed our last rays of hope, how Mr. Kothari had refused to help us and that no witnesses had appeared as yet. Daksh was initially hesitant about telling an outsider our family secrets, but eventually he came to accept Abhimanyu. Abhimanyu had a way with people—was it his gummy bears, his patience or simply his way of talking, I didn't know—but whatever it was, it seemed to work wonders. Abhimanyu was shocked to hear about the connection between D.P. Singh and Rajaji and sickened by the alarming levels of corruption that could cost an innocent person his life.

At Tihar, Inspector Khare was cold and unresponsive, so unlike his usual, friendly self. When we asked him if we could take a look at the forensic reports, he promptly refused. It was perplexing to see him like that, but soon the reason became clear. Commissioner D.P. Singh was at work.

Abhimanyu tried reasoning with Khare.

'Sir, we're mindful citizens. According to the Right to Information Act, we have a constitutional right to see the reports,' he said in his American accent.

Just as he said this, a rough voice came from behind us. 'Who is this barking American dog?'

We turned around to see a potbellied, unshaven police officer. His badge read, 'Commissioner D.P. Singh'.

'Excuse me?' Abhimanyu said angrily. Criticism was one thing, but being offensive was completely unacceptable.

'You want to see the report?' Singh taunted. 'They are with me. And you won't get them unless,' he gestured towards me with teasing eyes.

My lips quivered, but I kept a strong hold over myself.

'You rascal,' Abhimanyu said between clenched teeth. He was furious. I could see it in his eyes. He swung back to punch him hard in the face but Daksh caught his arm just in time. The same fire was burning inside him too.

He said to Abhimanyu in a firm voice while glowering at D.P. Singh, 'Now is not the time for this. We have work to get done.'

Abhimanyu took my hand and pressed it tightly. His veins throbbed in anger. I remembered that night in Yale when he had rescued me from the hooligans and my spirits lifted. I didn't need to be afraid of anything with him by my side.

'Oh, about your brother? I heard you lost your lawyer. Such a shame! You know it is a lost case, no one will take it up. No one sensible,' Singh provoked us further.

Then Daksh spoke.

'Mr. Commissioner D.P. Singh, get one thing straight in your head. The man that you've kept locked up inside that little cell of yours? There are very few like him, and he is innocent. And that is something I'm going to prove and show the world with or without your freaking reports. So if you'll excuse us, we need to go and meet him.'

And with that sentence he walked straight towards Arjun Bhaiya's cell with the two of us trotting close behind.

❧

Arjun Bhaiya was delighted to meet Abhimanyu.

'I must say I've heard quite a lot about you, young man,' he said.

'No you have not!' I interjected, self-consciously.

'Well, okay, not a lot. But you are the only one I've heard about from Yale so I guess that counts,' he teased.

Clearly Abhimanyu was enjoying this. After their little tete-a-tete, we began to talk about the real business.

'Bhaiya, Kothari turned out to be a serpent. He isn't taking up the case,' I told him worriedly.

'Oh. Now that's a little hurting,' Arjun Bhaiya said in a tone devoid of any emotion.

'Arjun, we need you to be more involved. You can't be so aloof!' Daksh cried out loud.

'Daksh, easy man,' interjected Abhimanyu.

There was an unperturbed look on Arjun Bhaiya's face. How could he remain calm while the rest of us were drowning in this whirlpool?

Then Abhimanyu said, 'He who has truth in his heart, needs no persuasion on his lips'.

Arjun Bhaiya was clearly impressed. 'Exactly. Because you see, if things don't get better today, there's always tomorrow. We will wait till the end.' Anyone could tell that he didn't mean a single word he was saying. This was not what the old Arjun would have said. And this wasn't the philosophy I was going to follow either.

'Oh so you mean we wait till everything's happy and okay on its own?' I demanded. 'Wait, flipping through a magazine? Wait, lying in bed, daydreaming? Well, no. That is not what we do. If things don't get okay, we fight. We fight for what is right, till the time we get what we want. What we deserve. We make it okay if it isn't, that's what we do.' There was grit and conviction in my voice.

'But whatever be the case, there's no way we can do anything, forget about winning, if we don't have a lawyer,' Daksh interjected.

'And there is no way we can achieve this with a government provided defence lawyer. In a country like India, I can only imagine how astute and skilful they will be.' Abhimanyu said, his disgust with the country resurfacing. We knew a lawyer was needed. But getting a lawyer now would not be an easy task. All the major newspapers and news channels had elaborated on the fact that Arjun Bhaiya was a brutal killer.

The havildar came to inform us that time was up. As we walked back, Inspector Khare came up to apologize for Singh's behaviour.

'Guys, I'm really sorry for Singh's behaviour. Though I'm new here, it has still been long enough to judge Singh. That man is an asshole. And to be honest how he behaved with you all wasn't even close to his truly bad behaviour. I think your friend,' pointing towards Abhimanyu, 'intimidated him. He is a scoundrel who's become the commissioner because that minister's daughter turned a blind eye to his follies and fell in love with him. He is so brazen that he appears on duty only once in a while.'

And then looking at Abhimanyu he added, 'I'm a mindful man too. But in a country like India, intelligent men are of little consequence. The autopsy reports of Harilal Mathur are in the confines of his office. I'm sorry; I won't be able to help you here.'

Abhimanyu smiled and said, 'Inspector Khare, in a country like India, intelligent men hardly exist. Had this not been the case, it wouldn't have been India. I read somewhere that even a fool recognizes that there is great sadness in a bucket of tears. But only a wise man thinks of conserving the water and use that bucket to wash his car.'

'And you're trying to imply that?'

'You're an intelligent man, you'll figure it out,' Abhimanyu said with a wink. 'If there is any information that you get regarding the case, please inform us sir.'

'I will,' replied Inspector Khare before we made a move.

THE TRAGEDY OF ERRORS

*D*aksh and I were at the breakfast table with Chachi dominating the scene when the landline rang. It was a bit of a shock, we didn't receive too many calls on the landline.

'Hello?' Daksh answered.

'Arjun Bedi's residence?' queried a young man.

'Yes, who is this?'

'That is irrelevant. I just want to tell you that I was there that day when the police officer collapsed.'

Daksh's bored expression perked up. His eyebrows almost reached the top of Mount Everest.

'What do you know about that day?'

'That Harilal Mathur did not die of a brain haemorrhage. As a matter of fact, he was not even hit by anything.'

'What? Is it true?'

'Every iota of it.'

'And how do you know this?'

'He was running after the protesters like the other police officers. But then, all of a sudden, he stopped and fell.'

'How do you know?'

'Because I was the one who called the ambulance and sent him to the hospital. As they were performing first-aid, one of the nurses said that there were no external injuries. What I'm essentially telling you is that the autopsy reports they are talking about on TV are incorrect. This information may help in saving Arjun.'

'I can't believe what you just said! By Jove! This is the best news I've ever heard! But why do you want to help Arjun at all? What will you gain from it?'

'Not all of us think like you, mister. Some of us actually want to help because we believe in goodness. Arjun is a very good man. The world needs leaders and examples to follow. That the path of righteousness leads you to prison is not the ideal we want to teach the next generation. I wanted to help so I helped. I'm going to put the phone down now and I expect you to keep this conversation to yourself. Best of luck.'

'Wait, who are you? What's your name?' Daksh asked frantically.

But the phone was disconnected.

Daksh's face turned red, his eyes were wide and his mouth had fallen open. His expression turned from surprise to disgust and then contempt. He didn't respond when I called out to him; he was in a daze.

'Daksh?' I called out aloud.

'He didn't die of a haemorrhage,' he said, disdain dripping from his words like melting ice.

'Those bastards lied to us. Arjun is being framed.'

'What?' I couldn't take in what he had just said. If Mathur hadn't died of a haemorrhage, then what did he die of?

Initially I was intrigued by this unexpected turn of events. Arjun Bhaiya had been framed wrongly! So all the jeers and insinuations that we had to face from insensitive neighbours and friends were without foundation. My blood boiled in fury! But what guarantee did we have that the man was telling Daksh the truth? And even if it was the truth, how would we be able to prove it without substantial evidence? We didn't even know where the man lived to get in touch with him. Forget his address; we didn't even know his name! How would we be able to prove the reports wrong? Oh my God! I never felt more helpless or frustrated! What a fool I was to build castles in the air!

Without saying another word, Daksh got up from the breakfast table, ran into the bedroom and returned with a backpack.

With a sadistic smile he said 'Rhea, let's get going. We have some ass to kick. Tell Abhimanyu to be waiting outside his hotel, we're picking him up in five minutes.'

Inspector Khare was traumatized when he heard the news about the fudged reports. Somewhere deep inside, he, too, must have known, but I let the thought slip; he was helping us out now by giving us Harilal Mathur's address.

Deep within Adhchini village, was a small flat. When we rang the bell, a haggard middle-aged woman peeped out.

'Y... Yes?' she stuttered apprehensively. Her red, tear-stained eyes showed fear.

'Mrs. Mathur?' I asked, knowing that the boys would worry her further.

'Yes. What do you want? Who are you?'

'I'm Rhea. We just wanted to ask you a few questions,' I said as politely as I could manage. To my surprise she shook her head in refusal and banged the door shut on my face.

Abhimanyu knocked next. In his pleasant American twang and patient voice, he said, 'Mrs. Mathur, we aren't from the police. We aren't from the government either. Our friend is in trouble, we need to save him. Please, we need your help.'

'No, I can't help you,' she said hastily through the door.

'But didn't your husband do that? Help people? He was a righteous police officer.' Abhimanyu appealed to her conscience. After a few minutes, she opened the door, her face solemn. A little boy of around seven or eight was jumping about, playing with a toy car, his father's police cap on his head.

'Zoooooooooom zooom zoooooooooooooooooooooom,' he went playfully, guiding the car over the modest sofa and the table in front of it. Daksh went up to him and bent down on his knees to look into his eyes.

'Hey, what's your name?' he asked.

'Karan,' said the boy continuing to play with his car.

'That's a nice car; you think I could play with you too?' Daksh asked.

'Okay,' Karan said running back inside a room, dragging Daksh by the finger.

Anyone who had met Daksh for the first time and observed his normal, cold manner would never have figured out his love for children. As a sister, I was gratified to see Daksh emerge from his hard shell and become a little boy himself.

'Hey, here,' Abhimanyu called out to Daksh. 'Give him these gummy bears,' tossing a packet of the Dollar Store candies.

In the meantime, Abhimanyu spoke to Mrs. Mathur.

'Mrs. Mathur,' he said in his courteous, gentlemanly manner, 'I know this is an excruciatingly painful time for you. To handle everything on your own isn't easy.'

'Yes, it is all very difficult, especially with Karan and his studies and everything,' Mrs Mathur said, wiping away a tear.

Daksh and Karan came out of the room. Holding out the packet of gummy bears to his mother, Karan said excitedly, 'Maa look what Bhaiya gave me! It is candy. Can I please have some? I know you told Papa not to have any sweet things, but I am a strong boy, I can have some, right?'

'Yes, you are a strong boy, you can have one Karan,' she said, forcing a smile.

'Mr. Mathur was diabetic?' Abhimanyu asked.

'Um… well, uh… yes. The doctor had told him to reduce his intake of sweets,' she answered hesitantly.

'Mrs. Mathur, you need to help us prove Arjun innocent. Even you know your husband wasn't murdered.'

'Beta, I am under immense pressure. I have been told to keep quiet about all this. I…' she was at a loss for words. Tears started streaming down her face as she fought to be strong. Mrs. Mathur's tears evoked a sense of empathy in me; but I couldn't break down now.

It's sad but true that the loss of a beloved person can never be replaced. It was easy for me to ask her not to cry and be strong but who would fill the void in her life now that her husband and the sole breadwinner was no more? Time the healer would surely fill the wounds, but I hoped she realized that what cannot be cured, must be endured.

Abhimanyu kept a comforting hand over her shoulder.

'Mrs. Mathur, had I been in your place, even I would have done the same. There is a lot of stress, don't hide your feelings, let your emotions out.'

'They said that they would give us compensation if I don't tell anyone anything. I need the money desperately. Karan is young. Hari was the only working member in our family. Without him I am left all alone.'

Her loud sobs filled the bare room as Abhimanyu tried to comfort her.

'Hari had a heart problem. Last year, we spent all our savings on his angioplasty. He was to get a stent in his heart soon. Every day I used to put a Sorbitrate in his pocket, just in case, you know. And then because of the campaigns and the People's Party movement, he was on duty for three consecutive days. It was obviously a strain. Even on that day I told him to stay at home and not report for duty, so much exertion was not good for him. But did he listen to me at all? He didn't. And there at India Gate, he had a cardiac arrest.'

She started sobbing uncontrollably. Daksh took Karan into another room to keep the innocent boy from seeing his mother break down.

'But please don't tell anyone I said this,' she sobbed.

'And so my brother has to bear the consequences of your fear!' Daksh shouted, coming into the room.

Abhimanyu fixed him with a stern look. The woman was still mourning the death of her husband.

'Mrs Mathur,' Abhhimanyu consoled her, 'We need to be strong in the face of adversity. Tell me, would your husband want you to hide the truth? An innocent life is at stake.'

'I realize that. I am a very god-fearing person, but I worry about the fate of my child.'

'Mrs. Mathur, they're firing the gun from your shoulder,' I spoke for the first time since entering in to the flat.

She looked at me earnestly and said, 'What other choice

do I have?'

Mrs Mathur told us her pitiful story. She was the eldest in a family of five girls and being from a conservative, lower middle-class background, her family had a tough time getting her married, since they could not afford a dowry. When her father received a proposal from Harilal, a government employee, a constable in the police force, he happily arranged her marriage to him immediately after she finished school. Now with her parents dead, she had nothing to fall back on except the compensation she would receive from the government. That was all she had to hold on to in life. Looking directly at us she said, 'My husband, I know, was honest, a man of integrity, a righteous person who stood by his convictions and advocated the truth, but I, on the other hand, do not have the courage to face the wrath of the government when they discover that I have not followed their instructions.'

I could see that she was caught between the devil and the deep sea. Her dilemma was "to help or not to", yet after dillydallying for a while she had made up her mind. Come what may... she needed to face the future with her head held high.

❦

We went back to the car, feeling lighter and happier.

'Guess what I have in here,' I said holding up my phone.

I pressed the play button on my phone; the entire conversation we had with Mrs. Mathur had been recorded.

'Aren't I smart?' I asked with a wink. I was extremely optimistic. In the past couple of days, I had been so overwhelmed by sorrow and depression that I'd forgotten what it was like to be happy. Now I could actually visualise Arjun Bhaiya being released from jail.

'Well, whose sister are you?' Daksh remarked. 'Look what I have in here.' He too, displayed his phone. While playing with Karan, Daksh had come across a prescription lying on the dining table. The large font read—Dr Subhash Arya, Cardiologist; Patient's name: Harilal Mathur. The prescription clearly proved that Harilal Mathur had recently had an echocardiography and the reports were not good. Susceptible to heart failure, he had been advised to cut down on sugar and salt and had been recommended a bunch of medicines to keep his blood pressure down as well. In this moment of joy, I looked up at Abhimanyu and batted my eyelids. He grinned naughtily and smacked me affectionately on my head. From his pocket he pulled out yet another packet of gummy bears and said teasingly, 'Precious things are packed in small packets.'

MEASURE FOR MEASURE

*A*anya was waiting for Daksh when we reached home. The TV was turned to a discussion on Arjun Bhaiya. Padma Shri Barkha Dutt, the eminent journalist known for her impartial reporting, was in conversation with Akul Nair.

'Daksh, Rhea, hi, I was waiting for the two of you,' she said the moment we walked in. She looked at Abhimanyu and gave him a warm smile.

'Hey,' Daksh said, giving her a hug and a peck on the cheek.

'Daksh, you didn't answer my call last night, I was worried. What's been going on? What happened to that Kothari lawyer?'

'He refused to take the case, Aanya.'

Genuine surprise and dismay was visible in Aanya's eyes. Then she brightened up.

'Rhea, I've always wanted to help you guys out in this. My father is a practicing lawyer.'

Now Daksh was surprised.

'Your father is a lawyer?' he asked, visibly puzzled.

'Well, yes. You mean you didn't know?'

'That's right. How would I know? You never told me your father was a lawyer!' Daksh shouted.

'Daksh!' I said sternly. 'What is wrong with you?'

He looked down, his eyes not meeting mine, or Aanya's.

'I.. I'm sorry,' he said.

Aanya walked over to him and stroked his hair.

'It's fine, I know the tension is getting to you Daksh,' she said, kissing his forehead.

I was standing right in front of Abhimanyu. Very casually, he put his arm around my waist. A pleasant shudder went through me. I looked back into the endless depths of his eyes and all I saw was honest goodness and care.

'Ahem, ahem,' Aanya grinned.

Immediately Abhimanyu let go of me and I started looking nonchalantly at the painting hung on the wall, pretending to study its composition.

'How about I take an appointment with Dad for you guys for Wednesday?'

'Sounds good,' I said happily.

❦

The bell rang. Mamma skipped in with a big grin on her face and a box of chocolates.

'Papa has started responding to stimuli! The doctors have shifted him from the ICU to a regular room. He should be discharged from the hospital soon,' she cried out in ecstasy. Her eyes sparkled with happiness. I felt relieved that Mamma had come back to life.

Despite the pressure and tensions weighing upon us, we had been carrying on with our activities. We had all been moving around like zombies, mechanically performing our daily chores, but at the back of our minds was always the nagging worry about our father. What a relief it was to hear this piece of good news. It looked like things were getting better now. The sun was beginning to shine in our lives once again after a long spell of despair, darkness and gloom.

∾

Daksh went to Dr. Arya's residence in New Friend's Colony to extract some additional information about Harilal Mathur. Dr. Arya was forthcoming and eager to help in whichever way he could. Mathur had been a regular patient of his and had a 70 per cent blockage in the main artery of his heart. The reports of his echocardiography clearly proved that if Mathur was unable to get a stent installed, he could succumb to a cardiac arrest. Just a few days before his death, he had complained of breathlessness and excessive sweating. Very generously, Dr. Arya handed over the reports to Daksh, for he too, wanted to see the right side win. And above all, he wanted to see this corrupt government collapse.

The following day, we visited Mr. Kapoor, Aanya's father and our potential lawyer. Mr. Kapoor was extremely responsive. He praised us for our courage and patience, our handling of such a challenging situation so well.

He said sympathetically, 'You all are young kids. And it wasn't fair on God's part to throw so much your way. But you know what they say, God never gives us more than we can handle. I am very proud of all of you. And Abhimanyu, Aanya told me about you. I think it's very gallant of you to come all this way to stand by your damsel in her distress!'

I could feel my cheeks getting hotter and hotter. I wondered if Abhimanyu was as mortified as I was.

'Well, chivalry is one quality I am glad I possess,' he retorted jokingly.

'Coming back to business, we have solid evidence. And there are no two ways about this case. We only need to look at the post-mortem report and then we're good to go!'

'Uncle, about those reports. The commissioner has concealed them,' Daksh said, sounding worried.

'But that's against the law! We'll file an application for the RTI.'

'Which I think will not be necessary,' I interjected assertively.

In response to the questioning looks that were shot at me, I said with a broad smirk, 'Aruna Roy is a very close friend of Jayshree Masi's.'

We had the reports, we knew the truth and we now needed the world to know this too.

The moment we got home, I rang up Masi. I knew she would be more than happy to help. It didn't take her even a second to call Aruna Roy and brief her about the case. In about five minutes, Aruna Roy gave me a call, assuring me that a copy of the report would be couriered to us. Those were the perks of being in contact with benevolent people. I cheerfully told Abhimanyu about the phone call, expecting some degree of approval, but he was anything but appreciative.

'That's the great thing about this country, right? Know people, get the work done. Don't know people, suffer,' he said flatly.

'Well, I... I guess I can't justify that,' I said, suddenly feeling deflated.

❧

The court's hearing was in two days time and we were well prepared. With all the evidence, including the post-mortem report which blatantly ignored the chronic heart failure angle, in favour of Bhaiya, we were confident of winning the trial. With one piece of good news came another: Papa had been shifted to a regular room after he had emerged from his coma! The doctors had said that they would keep him under observation for about a week, but medically he was perfectly healthy.

On the day of the court hearing just as Daksh and I were ready to leave, we were surprised to find Mamma, along with Bittu Chachi and Sonu Chacha waiting by the door. Mamma was looking her original self, she had applied her favourite red lipstick and was wearing a smart formal outfit. Suddenly everything was falling into place. All the broken pieces of the puzzle were fitting perfectly into place. Even Daksh was now fitting in.

When we reached the court, we saw Arjun Bhaiya dressed in civilian clothes, surrounded by a group of policemen. Mamma ran to him and covered him with kisses and tears. She was meeting him for the first time after Papa had fallen sick. She'd had no contact with him for more than three weeks and the pleasure of seeing him again filled her with immense joy. Arjun Bhaiya was a Mamma's boy. Because we were younger, he always seemed mature and responsible to us, but here in his Mamma's arms, he became her little boy again.

The trial lasted for just under an hour. It was no surprise that the court's order was in Bhaiya's favour. The facts were presented to the judge and it took him no time to undo the wrong that had been done to Arjun Bedi. The court also convicted Commissioner D.P. Singh for the misuse of power while in a position of authority and violating the Right to Information by refusing to display government documents. This was not expected from a man holding such a responsible position. It was a blot on Indian democracy, such unscrupluous twerps needed to be weeded out so that India could be free of corruption. So that Satyamev actually Jayate.

MIDNIGHT'S DREAM

*W*ith Mamma's permission, Abhimanyu took me out to dinner at the Taj Mahal Hotel. I wore a peach sequinned dress that I'd worn for my prom the previous year. I blow-dried my hair into perfect bouclé and painted my eyes with a shade of pink. I wanted the evening to be perfect and for perfect I had to look perfect. Punctual as ever, Abhimanyu reached at 7.30 pm. He was wearing a black corduroy coat with ripped blue jeans which I always used to find ugly. But today the ripped jeans didn't look all that bad; they looked good. I came outside shyly. I felt self-conscious. Was I over-dressed? Was my makeup too much? Oh! I felt weird in my tummy.

It was a weekday and there were very few people around. He escorted me to a secluded table in the open. The moonlight cast a soft glow over us and soft, sensuous music was playing in the background. I felt as if we were the stars of a romantic Bollywood film. The candle's yellow light flickered in Abhimanyu's eyes; I was already drowning in their golden glow. The scent of jasmine wafted across sensuously. It was a perfect night, with a perfect companion. None of us spoke for a while. We hadn't found ourselves in such a romantic situation before. The silence became awkward. Suddenly Abhimanyu stood up. Much to my surprise, he took an ice cube from the ice bucket, placed it on the ground and crushed it loudly with his foot. He looked down into my eyes. It seemed as if time stopped still as he got down on his knees. My mind became fuzzy. I couldn't focus; what was happening? Then he smiled. And in his smile I saw something more beautiful than roses, more beautiful than the stars, more beautiful than beauty itself. He bent down and whispered something in my ear. His soft lips brushed against my hair. I felt my knees shake. He pulled a strand of my hair out of my eye and placed it gently behind my ear. I could have died then. Literally. I couldn't breathe; my heart stopped beating completely; my entire body was paralysed by his touch. Slowly and softly he said, 'Now,' he paused, 'now that the ice is broken, let me tell you that... that... I hoped that your dress would be shorter.'

The ass.

Ugh.

I should have known that something like this was coming.

'You are an ass,' I said, punching him playfully on his shoulder.

He laughed his usual carefree laugh; the one that had always made me stop and listen to.

'And you,' I said in mock accusation, 'were doing that just to draw closer to me, because otherwise you knew you wouldn't stand a chance!'

'Oh!' he cried, acting hurt, 'If it be a sin to covet thy honour, I am the most offending soul.'

'A most notable coward, an infinite and endless liar, an hourly promise breaker, the owner of no one good quality,' I teased him further with a wink.

'Hey, now that's being unfair,' he said catching hold of my fingers.

My heart skipped a beat. My face burned. There was no need for me to have applied that blusher, natural blush would have sufficed. I looked around; at the waiter standing in the distance, the other couple sitting at a little distance from us, everywhere but at Abhimanyu. A strand of my hair fell on my face. I let it be there, thankful that it hid the cherry shade I had turned. Then, with his eyes earnest, he said, 'I knew the second I met you that there was something about you I needed. Turns out it wasn't just something, it was all of you.'

His deep, dark eyes stayed locked with mine. His hold on my fingers tightened. I never loved him more than I did in that moment.

'Abhimanyu,' I said cautiously. I wasn't sure how to put it, but I thought it was important for him to hear this from me. 'You truly are the merchant of "vain ice" considering the fact that it's so difficult to break. I'm supposed to be the one with the "shy locks". I sometimes feel like an ant, an ion in front of your *abhimaan*.'

'Rhea, I'm falling. Hold on to me! I'm falling in love with you!'

Fireworks went off inside me. And the heat they produced was clearly pouring out from my burning ears and cheeks. It was then that I realized how hopelessly in love I was with him.

THE CAESAR

*N*amrata, Mamma's cousin's daughter from Varanasi, was getting married in a few days. Namrata Di was an Economics Honours student from Delhi University and had graduated at the top of her class. Because of Papa's health issues, Mamma could not attend her wedding, but she insisted that Daksh, Arjun Bhaiya and I had to go for we couldn't run away from social obligations. She was also keen that Arjun Bhaiya take a short vacation away from Delhi after all his trials and tribulations. As Abhimanyu would be in Delhi for three more days and Varanasi happened to be his hometown, we asked him to join us. The last fifteen days had been a rollercoaster ride for him as well, and we needed some time to unwind and relax. What could be better than a Punjabi wedding? I had assumed that Abhimanyu would be enthusiastic about the whole programme, particularly since he could meet his family and friends in Varanasi. But oddly, it seemed like he was forcing himself to come along. He agreed only because I had insisted using emotional blackmail. Packing our bags with heavy traditional outfits and jewellery, the four of us set off for Varanasi. During the hour-long plane ride, Abhimanyu just stared out the window looking dismal. He quickly wiped away a stray tear from his eyes. I wondered what secrets Varanasi held to make Abhimanyu so vulnerable? I didn't want to embarrass him by trying. Sometimes silence and time were the best medicine. Abhimanyu didn't speak a word till we reached the sacred grounds of the city of Kashi. Nidhi Mami, Namrata Di's mother, had sent a car for us. We squeezed uncomfortably into the small Alto and started off for the wedding house. The road leading from the airport to the city was narrow and lined with shacks. There was hardly any greenery, instead there was trash everywhere—the roads, the ghats, the entrance to the temples. Thin, scantily-clad children lurked about the streets, knocking at car windows hoping to secure a coin or two. A group of religious sages draped in saffron crossed us chanting holy hymns and, to my horror, smoking cigarettes!

I turned to Abhimanyu and asked, 'Do you remember all of this?'

'This place hasn't changed a bit in all these years,' he said rather grimly. 'The same poverty, the same old hypocritical, sanctimonious sadhus, the same filth, all coutinue to reside in this place.'

'Hypocritical?'

'Well most certainly. The saffron flags flying in every nook and cranny of this city try to create a sacred atmosphere. And they are pretty convincing to the outsider too. But only those who live here know that this is merely a façade.'

I was right as always. India was a bottomless pit, propelling further into an endless hell of immorality and sin and sucking into its whirlpool every wandering soul. I understood now why the dirt that colonised the roads and the corners could never be done away with. It was His way of drawing a parallel with the muck and filth that filled the people's hearts and minds. Even after so many years, the parasites continued to breed rampantly.

We reached the wedding venue, ablaze with glittering lights and blaring music. Red and gold drapes covered the whole banquet area, with strands of jasmine and marigold outlining the stairs. Young children and elderly ladies were dancing to peppy Bollywood tunes. As we entered, we were welcomed with a series of over-enthusiastic hugs and greetings from people we had never met before. I was hoping to find some cousin or acquaintance in the midst of this teeming crowd of people. Jayshree Masi, who was supposed to be there, was nowhere to be seen. The four of us felt pretty awkward standing around, doing nothing but observing fat aunties dance the bhangra. A delicious smell of frying *jalebis* filled the air. The men had conveniently settled themselves by the bar, their wives looking anxious for a while until they moved to the dance floor. The ear-splitting sound of the *dhol* added the much-needed Punjabi touch to the wedding. It only stopped when Namrata Di, resplendent in her exquisite Indian bridal gown, descended the stairs. The stereo began to play a sentimental wedding folksong, causing an outburst of tears. Fed up of simply standing around, watching people dance and cry, Arjun Bhaiya went to get some food to fill our empty stomachs. Actually, he just needed to escape from any Mami or Masi who could come to interrogate him. Not out of concern but just to satisfy a craving for gossip. After which they could feel smug that their children were doing better than Mrs. Bedi's geniuses. To pry and embarrass people seems to be a popular pastime, and I'm amazed by the probing questions that relatives and friends keep asking. There was an Aunt Rosy who had the audacity to say, 'We bring children into this world

with so many expectations, only to see this day of ignominy...
What a shame!'

As Daksh, Abhimanyu and I were trying to entertain
ourselves by eavesdropping on other people's conversations, we
heard a woman brag about her new gold bracelet.

'I know ji, this one cost me eighty-five grand. And 22-carat
gold. Pretty, isn't it? I told my husband, charity begins at home.
Why throw away useful money to some NGO or ashram? These
people are big thieves anyway. Instead, invest in jewellery.'

Another one gushed over her daughter's "Manish Malhotra"
sari which she had bought in Mumbai.

Another, '*Hayo rabba*! The *dhol wala* was pathetic! Paaji, if
you're over with your drink-shrink, shall we have some food-
shood?' was a humorous treat to the ear.

'Namrata is such a lucky girl to have found a match like
Pranay!'

'Did you know that Devji, Namrata's father, has given two
cars as dowry? Only then did they get such a wonderful *rishtha*!'

Madness seemed to be bursting out of every corner and
the bling was starting to hurt my eye! The loud *baraatis* were
battling the previous night's hangover.

*I was disgusted. Disgusted by the hollowness and triviality
of the people. In the 21st century, fathers still have to pay huge
dowries to get their daughters married into decent families! Such
extravagance! Holding such huge functions where half of the people
are unknown to the bride and groom.*

'Rhea,' Abhimanyu said to me. From his expression I
gathered that he was repulsed by what he saw and heard. I
was ready for another lecture on India and the Indian mentality.
'This country has not changed. You all talk about modernity,

advancement in every sphere, but you are still so shallow and narrow-minded that you believe in the dowry system, exploiting the girls who are equally educated.'

'Abhimanyu, if your blood boils with anger, it's time you took action. Be the change you want to see in the world! It's easy to criticize and find faults, all of us can do that and we do. But the person who channelises his criticism into a cause is the one we call a hero.'

We finally found Masi. Arjun Bhaiya had been waiting to meet her. Had she not helped us contact Aruna Roy, our plea for the reports would have been answered only in our next lives. I was excited too; I wanted her to meet Abhimanyu who had helped us emerge from this impenetrable *chakravyuh*.

'Looks can be deceptive Abhimanyu,' I said, pointing to Masi, 'She may look frail and petite, but she has an iron will and the passion to excel in everything! Believe me when I say that she is an epitome of energy and the personification of perfection.' Jayshree Masi was one person I could go on talking about! She was the Statue of Liberty holding up the torch and showing me the way.

'Good evening, uhh, mam,' Abhimanyu approached her awkwardly.

'I run a school; I think I have enough people calling me mam. Aunty would probably do better,' Masi joked with him, trying to make him more at ease with her. Her boundless energy and exuberance could be intimidating at times.

He laughed and said conversationally, 'I've heard about you.'

'I hope all good things,' she chuckled.

'Of course!'

'How are you liking Varanasi?'

'I'm contemplating whether it's a city of messiahs or the mafia.'

'Oh, that's a little harsh, though unfortunately true,' she nodded in agreement.

'I know, right? Here in India, nobody seems to care. "Seems" is probably not the right word, I know for a fact that they don't. It's always about themselves, their good and their gain. It's as if morals and ethics don't exist at all! We study the *Mahabharata*, yet don't imbibe anything from it.'

Jayshree Masi replied in her wise and patient way, 'Abhimanyu beta, there are many who work selflessly to change this facet of India. Aruna Roy, you know of her I'm sure, left her prestigious IAS post to serve the humble poor. It takes different kinds of people to constitute this world. And it's not fair to bracket them all as corrupt and selfish. We must fight against the unwieldy government machinery. Instead of losing hope, we need to have the conviction and confidence to bring about a change ...however small it may be.'

Abhimanyu continued, 'These small changes are often decimated by unnecessary acts of skulduggery and sleaze. The People's Party with Akul Nair initially impressed many by their vision and philosophy. But soon enough I realised that they were no different from the rest. Their *bhook hartals* and Nair's refusal to accept security are not helping India in the race for development. I followed him when Arjun's case was going on. The People's Party's ideology is appropriate but their execution is outrageous! It's the 21st century for god's sake! *Bhook hartals,* sitting on roads or refusing security is not going to lead anyone anywhere. Take for example, providing free electricity and water to the poor. What are you getting at? You're only making them more indolent by offering them a platter full of goodies! And who is paying for their share of electricity? The ones who actually work? Huh, it's funny how simple economics doesn't hit these people! Forget politics for the moment, what about the average citizen? Look at the litter and filth. Look at the Ganga River. The Ganga is supposed to be a sacred river, but today, all I see is a stream of slurry. And in the last four years that I've been away, nothing has changed. Not a trace!'

Abhimanyu's tone was resolute. But there was something else in his voice too. Anger. And frustration. He wanted to see his country change. A fire of passion burnt in him. It was then that I realized that he didn't hate his country; he loved it dearly. Just the way over-protective parents prevented their kids from taking the wrong path, he couldn't stand to see India drowning in a quagmire of filthy corruption.

'It is rather easy for you from the developed western world to come and judge India, but you are ignorant of what India is,' Masi said earnestly. 'Don't be dismayed by the filth on the roads, open sewers and drains, the half-naked beggars, the red tapism. People who dine in five-star hotels won't know about terrible hunger, sleeping on footpaths, walking miles to fill a bucket of water. Every public service in this country is strained to its breaking point. Today's youth is not corrupt, it's people like Arjun and Rhea, and you too for that matter, who are committed to make a difference. We don't smell the roses as yet, but there's a change in the air which a keen observer will be able to discern. India is a very diverse country, with people belonging to different castes, religions, regions and thus mindsets. With such vast diversity, it is obvious that there will be differences, conflicts and problems. These are the dissimilarities that need to be integrated. What have you given to the country to expect anything in return? Young man, if you have any mettle in you stop looking down at the current situation, be a part of this revolution to change India's landscape.'

After Masi's long speech, Abhimanyu's face fell, bleached of colour. He had a lump in his throat and his body was tight with tension. His whole demeanour was one of helplessness. I am certain he knew what Masi said was right. As citizens of India, as Indians, we all have a responsibility towards our country. And failure to live up to those responsibilities is what has led to the deterioration of our nation.

LOVE'S LABOUR LOST

That night after the wedding celebrations when the bride was bidding adieu to her family, I stole a glance at Abhimanyu who sat solemnly by the window staring out at the Ganga. *Diyas* were afloat, illuminating the river in an auspicious glow. At least a thousand people had come to the banks to absolve themselves of their sins. It was then that the river seemed truly sacred. I went and sat next to Abhimanyu quietly.

'It's beautiful, isn't it?' I asked, gazing outside.

He nodded, and then said in an amused but cynical tone, 'A perfect example of how pretentious this world can be. This place is where life and death actually converge.'

His red eyes told me something wasn't right. And the sardonic huff which followed verified that.

'Abhimanyu?' I said softly.

'Yeah?'

'Can I ask you something?'

'Unhuh,' he said, still in a trance.

'Why do you hate India so much? I thought coming to Varanasi would give you a chance to meet with your family and friends, but you haven't done that. What happened?'

He looked at me meaningfully. For the first time I felt his

defences going down. His eyes revealed more than words could express. They were a window into his soul, and something was smouldering in there.

'You want to know what happened?' he said with pained eyes though he faked a smile.

'Yes. I do.'

'My dad was an industrialist. I was eight when some rogues kidnapped him and killed him. And then for what? Money? Land? To keep me away from the distressing situation, my mom sent me to boarding school.'

I was dumbstruck. My face went slack. My mouth opened but I couldn't utter a word. And I had believed that life had been unfair to us!

'So, this is the story of my life,' he said.

'Abhimanyu... I...' I fumbled, not finding the right words.

'They kept him in captivity for over three months and when we couldn't pay the exorbitant ransom, they simply killed him.' As he turned towards the lit river, his eyes glistened as he fought to be strong. 'It was a long time ago. My memories aren't as vivid and the pain not so severe. Just coming back here. to where it all happened, brought back those memories.'

'I'm so sorry.' I said, feeling terrible for not being able to do anything. 'But, I don't understand, why would anyone do that?'

He gave a sarcastic laugh; it was bitter and cold. 'If only I knew.'

'And where is your mom now?' I asked, considering he hadn't gone to meet her in Varanasi.

'She lives in Chicago now with her sister. I don't blame her for running away. In some part of her mind, she still blames herself for what happened. For not being able to raise the money to save Dad. The least she desires and deserves is not to be reminded of that time.'

'I'd like to meet her someday,' I said in an attempt to change the subject.

'Yeah, I'd want you to meet her too,' Abhimanyu said, his deep-set eyes now fixed on mine.

At that point, Arjun Bhaiya waved to us as the *doli* was leaving.

❧

Abhimanyu was to fly back to the US the next day. And soon, the next day was today.

All his bags were packed and placed outside; his ticket and passport in his hands. He was going back. Back to the land where he thought he belonged. My heart felt empty. I had known he would go, but the thought hadn't struck me that I would never see him again. It hurt. It hurt as much as it did when Bhaiya was implicated. As much as it had when Papa went into a coma. Or maybe a little more than that. Abhimanyu came home to say goodbye to Arjun Bhaiya, Daksh and my parents. On his way out he even had a word with Chachi, who had fantasized about him getting married to her Dolly, and promised he'd look for a suitable boy for her daughter in the US. He had become an integral part of our family over the past few days; it was hard to imagine life without him anymore. I tried very hard to contain myself but my eyes were brimming over with tears.

Daksh and I went to the airport to drop off Abhimanyu. Daksh rarely got along with anyone. He was choosy about the people he wanted to make friends with. He had endured Abhimanyu for many days without complaining or cribbing even once; that said a lot about his affection for Abhimanyu.

As we reached the airport, Daksh told me to accompany Abhimanyu till the gate while he would wait in the car. It was embarrassing to have your brother suggest indirectly that you could have a moment alone with the man you love.

'Abhimanyu,' I said with whatever little hope I had left, 'don't go.'

'I have to Rhea. I don't want to spend my life here in India. I can't. Let me take you away with me to the US. We'll live in New Haven and go to New York on the weekends. I want to take you to the Niagara Falls. I want to take you surfing in Hawaii. I want you to see the world from the top of the Empire State Building. Come with me, Rhea. I want you, I need you,' Abhimanyu implored.

'Abhimanyu, there is a lot I need to do here,' I said.

'You can do the same there too.'

'But my country needs me more. This country needs you too. The cause is always greater than the people, Abhimanyu.'

'This country is incorrigible.'

'Haven't you heard the story of Abhimanyu? He entered the deadly *chakravyuh* knowing that he did not have the expertise to get beyond the seventh circle. But his valour and determination to win the war did not allow him to succumb to the fear that he was incompetent or the task insurmountable. Abhimanyu was the most illustrious of the Pandavas and the Kauravas. Stay Abhimanyu, you were born to make a difference. We have surely been victorious in one battle, but there are many more to go. All is not hunky-dory. There will be hundreds of Mahabharatas in the future and we need more Abhimanyus and Arjuns to combat them.'

'Rhea…'

I smiled in understanding and said, 'Follow your heart. Go where it takes you.'

The loss of parting was immense, but then the course of true love never did run smooth.

I hugged him for the last time, but he quickly pulled away. He turned away his face, but not before I saw the tears in his eyes.

He pushed his trolley inside, leaving me alone with my emotions. Dark clouds had gathered and streaks of lightning lit up the skies. It was going to be a stormy night.

ALL'S WELL THAT ENDS WELL

I walked into the airport to see hordes of people trying to find their way around. The thunder outside reflected my tumultuous thoughts. Rhea's words rang in my mind like temple bells triggering an awakening. What happened to my father was wrong and I've hated India enough for that. But I was here now, in India. Four years of studying Political Science in Yale should benefit the country that fed me, bred me and bore me. Someone told me that if I wanted to see toilets being built before temples, then I must make those toilets. America is a beautiful country without any doubt, and even today if asked whether I love it, I'd say yes without a moment of hesitation. But one can't always reside in beauty; we need to learn how to grow a lotus in of a swamp. When so many can leave their white-collar jobs in the US to serve their motherland, why shouldn't I? Rhea was right; I was and I am Abhimanyu and this time I know how to tackle the seventh chakra. I looked back at the gates. They beckoned me. I had to go back—to Rhea, to my country. Lifting my suitcase, I ran back bumping into an old lady, a police officer; and finally I was out of the gate moving towards the love of my life.

I stood alone outside the airport, hoping for some miracle to happen, hoping for him to turn back. But who was I trying to fool? The joke would be on me anyway. I called Daksh to tell him that I was ready to go home.

He burst out of the door like a strong gust of cold wind. Before I saw him coming, his arms were wrapped tightly around me as he pulled me close to him and his lips touched mine. Softly. His forehead touched mine as he whispered into my ear, 'I love you. And I can't live without you.'

'Abhimanyu, you're not going?' I asked wiping away the tears of happiness.

Instead of answering my question, he bent down on one knee and said, 'Rhea Bedi, believe me when I say that there cannot possibly be a girl more beautiful, goofy, silly, likeable, and vivacious than you. Really. And I'm totally in awe of you. I want to be the person in your life who makes you smile, the one you go through thick and thin with, I want to be the one who gets you gummy bears, the one whose shoulder you cry on. And I'd do anything to be that guy, the guy who will own your heart forever and ever.'

'You already are that guy, Abhimanyu. And you have been that guy for longer than you think you have,' I said.

'Well then, Sin from thy lips? O trespass sweetly urged! Give me my sin again,' he inclined his face towards mine mischievously, inviting a jokey whack on his head.

ACKNOWLEDGEMENTS

Writing this book was like a car journey—there were bumps that deflated the tyres; roads that led to nowhere; traffic jams that instilled in me a sense of banality. But with the help of certain mechanics who fixed the faults, the cops who guided me through the traffic and the passers-by who gave me the correct directions, I finally reached my destination. And without further ado, I'd like to thank all those who made the completion of this journey possible.

To Swati Jiji, without whose constant motivation and support, my engine would've ceased. Thank you for believing in me when I didn't, for encouraging me to write that one last draft again, for pushing me forward at every step and for always being there.

To Jayshree Masi, whose enthusiasm and reassurance drove me forward. Thank you for those endless talks and discussions, for being that inspiration and steering me forward.

To Morris Mam, whose guidance and expertise were invaluable. To Mamma and Papa, without whose patience and pampering this book would not have been possible at all. Thank you for tolerating my tantrums, for staying up nights with me, for being that pillar of support that gave me the strength and will to not give up till the end.

To Rupa Publications India, who gave me the confidence to be what I am today. Thank you for providing me with a platform I could never have imagined myself on.

To each and every one who made this dream possible. Thank you. Thank you. Thank you.